Jag

Black Hawk MC
Book Five

by Carson Mackenzie

Published by CM Books, LLC
Copyright © November 2018 Carson Mackenzie
Cover Design by Carson Mackenzie
Cover Images Licensed for Use: Deposit Photos
ISBN# 978-1-952184-34-5
ISBN# 978-1-078746-72-4
ISBN# 978-1-710347-16-6

Synopsis

Dominic "Jag" Amara is calm, cool, and always in control. Being the club's attorney and its VP, he needs to be. People depend on him. But he finds it all tested every time he comes in contact with a certain redhead. She pushes buttons he didn't even know he possessed.

River Ramey is starting over with a new town, a new job, a new life. She needs and deserves it. What she doesn't need are the feelings the arrogant biker brings out in her. She has already gotten rid of one man who tried to control her and has no plans to get tied up with another. No matter how attracted she is to him.

As River and Jag spend time together, their pasts come calling—can they handle what the past stirs up—or will they let it pull them in different directions?

Table of Contents

Prologue

Jag

The door to my townhouse closed with a slam worthy to shake the pictures on the wall, then the clicking of heels on the wood floor echoed throughout. I closed my laptop and leaned back in the chair and waited.

"I can't believe you're going through with this," Simone said as she waltzed into the kitchen and stopped in front of me. Not a hello, a kiss, or even a fuck you. Nope, straight to jumping my shit. But it was what I expected out of her.

"What part of I've decided to resign my commission, did you not understand?"

Simone's hands went to her hips, and she glared at me. How the hell had I put up with this woman for three months? The only redeeming quality she held was her adventurous nature in bed. She was always up for anything. Though that was growing old with her.

"Nothing. I figured you would come to your senses about being a small town attorney for some motorcycle club. I thought we shared something special. That's why I asked Daddy about you working for him. He called and said you turned down his offer at the firm." She jerked her head, and the move tossed her blond hair over her shoulder. Like I hadn't seen that move a hundred times.

The offer from her dad had been a great one. Top salary and a junior partnership with full partner in five years. Any attorney would have salivated over the proposal; however, I knew it wasn't my experience that brought the interest in me. It was the woman who stood in front of me whose daddy indulged her every whim.

Simone was a spoiled twenty-four-year-old woman who had never held a job. She'd been twelve when her mother died from ovarian cancer, leaving her dad a single parent with a daughter entering her teenage years.

"Did you listen to anything when we talked last week? I'm going back to Shades Valley, Washington. It's my home. And it isn't *some* motorcycle club, it is *my* club. I never planned to be away permanently, Simone. Do you recall any of that conversation?" I asked, and she rolled her brown eyes. I wasn't sure what I'd expected from her; in the last week, Simone's behavior had changed. After telling her my plans, she began hinting about how she didn't know if she could live away from her dad. That if *we* stayed in DC, we could have a fantastic life.

Not sure what brought on her line of thinking because I'd not once mentioned she and I were headed toward that type of commitment. Hell, I hadn't asked her to join me in Washington. She knew the deal when we started going out because I told her. I never planned to settle anywhere other than Washington. The Navy was temporary, as were the women who passed through my life. There had been no deception on my part other than a mutual companionship, nothing was going to lead into anything permanent. Each woman I dated knew that it was exclusive between the two of us until one of us was ready to move on. I found over the years that honesty, in the beginning, helped with hurt feelings in the end. Or at least minimized them.

Simone and I met at one of the many Navy functions the Judge Advocates had to attend. She'd come with her father, who was once the college roommate of the DJAG (Deputy Judge Advocate General). Hobnobbing with the brass was the part of the job I despised, but I played my role well.

Now I planned to not only do what I loved—but live in a place I loved as well. My stint in the Navy had taught me a lot, but it was time for me to move on.

Simone placed a hand on my shoulder and moved closer. Watching her face, I knew when she decided to try a different tactic to get me to comply.

"Oh, Dominic," she purred and straddled my lap, "won't you rethink Daddy's offer? We can visit your club whenever you want and still have a life here—together." She bent her head and ran her tongue up my neck and circled my ear while she rubbed her tits against my chest. "We are so... good together. Do I need to remind you just how good? Take me here. Any. Way. You. Want." She ground her hips down for emphasis while she continued to kiss and nibble down my neck.

A part of me wondered just how far she would go to convince me to stay, but considering I hadn't even hardened from her gesture, it would be a waste of time. Besides, I may be an asshole, but that didn't mean I would nail her in my kitchen, then boot her out the door.

I grabbed a handful of her hair and pulled until she stopped what she was doing and leaned away. Whatever her endgame, I was done playing. No reason to drag out the inevitable.

"Up," I said, and moved to give her no other choice than to stand. I let go of her hair as she lifted off me. I stood along with her, took a deep breath, and prepared for the next scene because with women like Simone, there was always a next one when they didn't get their way.

"We are perfect together. We could have everything if you would just think about it," she said, and pouted. I once thought the move was cute. Once. Now, I was disgusted more with myself than with her for letting my lower region rule.

"I'm leaving as soon as the Navy releases me. It's a done deal, Simone. I have no plans or desire to stay here. When we got together, I never hid the fact the Navy nor a prestigious job were in my long-term plans. As for us... I told you point blank that I wasn't the relationship long haul guy. You told me you understood, and you weren't looking to be tied down either. But even knowing, you took it upon yourself to have your daddy offer me a job."

"Please, men always say they aren't looking to get tied down. But when two people get along like we do, it is the next step. But you won't give us a chance. You can't even keep a commitment to the Navy. And you know what? You'll be nothing without me." She cocked her hip and placed a hand on it. Her expression said she was gearing up for a good show. One I had no desire to purchase a ticket for.

Christ, what the fuck was I thinking? Yeah, she had wanted to take the relationship to the next level by moving in with me after a month. As I looked at Simone, I inwardly groaned. I so didn't want to deal with any of this.

"I gathered the few items you've left here. They're by the front door. Come on, I'll see you out and carry the box to your car." I started out of the kitchen, and a crash followed my exit. By the sound, it seemed I would be purchasing a new laptop.

I kept walking and hoped she'd have the tantrum out of her system before we were outside. As I bent to pick the small box up, something hit the wall above my head. Pieces of glass rained down on the floor along with a wooden frame, then a photo floated to join the debris. I reached for the photograph, and my brothers' faces stared back at me.

We'd taken the picture in front of the clubhouse before the six of us went our separate ways. I couldn't help but grin because I knew if they were here, they would enjoy the hell out of themselves at my expense.

"You're a fucking bastard, Dominic!" Simone yelled as I rose and turned in time to receive a slap to my cheek. When she moved her hand back to do it again, I balanced the small box under one arm and caught her wrist in my other hand before she could land it.

"I'll give you the first one, darlin'. But that's all you'll get. Enough."

"My father knows many people. He'll ruin you in that podunk town, along with your precious club."

"Oh, darlin', he won't. Because unlike you, he knows that every action comes with a consequence and your daddy is too smart of a man. Besides, my club's reach is a lot longer than his. Now, think of the nice European vacation you'll be able to work out of him for this," I said and let go of her wrist to open the door. It wouldn't be the first time the man paid for her to go overseas on a whim. He'd paid for her to go to Naples, Italy, when I was sent on a two-week assignment there. All because she whined about missing me. And that had taken place less than a month after we met. Imagine my surprise when she showed up, then when we came back, she started dropping hints about moving in together.

I should've cut her loose then. Never again. Hot, sweaty sex be damned.

I moved to the front door. The sooner this was done, the better. But Simone wasn't quite finished.

"Go, but you'll realize what you lost."

"Doubtful," I mumbled under my breath as I stepped out the door, then down the two steps to the sidewalk that led to the driveway on the side of the townhouse. I reached her car before she had made it out of the door.

When she stepped down to the sidewalk, she popped the trunk with her key fob, and I set the box inside. By the time I closed the trunk, she stood at the driver's side door.

"I always thought your laid-back demeanor was a wonderful trait. Instead, I think you use it to cover up the bastard underneath," Simone sneered, pulled the driver's side door open and slid into her car. "And know this—you'll find no one like me, and while you're regretting your poor decision because you will, I will be in another man's arms and his bed." She slammed the car door on her parting words. The engine turned over, and I stepped quickly to the side. Frankly, I wouldn't put it past her to clip me with the vehicle.

After I watched her drive away, I turned toward the front of my place, and that's when I noticed the car parked at the curb with a man leaning on the hood. His dark hair touched his shoulders, and he had his arms crossed over his chest. The smirk and cocked eyebrow told me he had heard most of the exchange between Simone and me.

"Christ, the man whose bed she lands in, you really should send a condolence card to him," he said as he dropped his arms, pushed off the hood, and started toward me. "Shit, brother, were you that desperate for a woman?"

When he reached the sidewalk and stood in front of me, we clasped hands, then I pulled him in for a hug.

"Goddamn, it's good to see you. But aren't you a little far from Bragg?"

Coast grinned and shook his head. "Landed at Dulles earlier and thought I would stop by since I was in the area. Going to be around DC for a couple of days before I head back to base."

"Should I even bother to ask where you've been?" I asked and got another smirk for an answer.

"Nah, you know the deal. If I share, I'd have to kill you," Coast said, and I snorted; it was something he always said when asked about anything to do with his job. Then again, being Delta Force, who knew if that shit was true or false.

"Got time to stay and have some dinner with me?"

"Sure do. Even have more time than that. Thought I'd crash here until I have to fly out if it's alright with you?"

"As you saw, my evening freed up, and I don't have anything planned for the next couple of days. It *is* the weekend. I'm sure we can find a few things to do."

"So, since you're free, why don't we go inside and order takeout? Then we can sit and drink a few beers while you fill me in on what I witnessed," Coast said, and I grinned.

"Well shit, we'll need more than a few beers if I'm going to talk about Simone," I said as we stepped through the front door of my place. "Watch your step, I've got a small mess to clean up."

Coast chuckled and shook his head when he glanced at the broken picture frame laying on the floor.

"Damn," he said when we reached the kitchen, and I bent to pick the busted laptop off the floor. "Oh yeah, definitely need to the hear the story about that woman. Then when we're done with that, you can tell me if the rumor about you resigning your commission and heading home has any merit." Coast slapped me on the back, then pulled out a chair and sat.

"Fuck, my dad didn't waste any time." I sat the broken computer on the bar, then opened the fridge, pulled out two beers, and handed one to Coast.

"Not when he's excited, brother. Your pops didn't mention the others to you?" Coast asked as I joined him at the table after I grabbed the takeout flyers in the drawer.

"No, we talked about what I needed for the Washington Bar. I want to be cleared to practice in the state as soon as possible. Why? Did something happen?"

"Where to begin. Well, Crusher's clearing base now. Flirt is out on a mission, but whenever he gets back, he's not going to re-up. Devil is back at his base after another stint in Afghanistan and has a little over two months left on his commitment before he calls it quits. Speed is the only one my dad didn't have news on." Coast leaned back and took a drink of his beer.

"Speed just left for Iraq a couple months ago. He visited me the weekend before he deployed. Since he lost his dad, it's been rough on him, brother. Even being in the same vicinity as each other, I only see him every once in a while. I don't know about you, but I can't imagine going back to the club and my dad not being there," I said, and Coast agreed.

We sat in silence for a minute, and I'm sure Coast was thinking the same as I was. Cutter's death had brought not only sadness to the entire club, but our dads had changed after his death. Losing their friend and brother hit them hard. They talked more about turning the club over to the six of us when we came home. And by what Coast said, it looked like they were going to get their wish sooner than they probably counted on.

"You mentioned the others, but what about you, Coast?" I asked and shoved the takeout menus toward him.

"This was my last assignment with my team. I'm out of the rotation, and my replacement is already at Bragg and raring to go. I'll start clearing when I get back. If the transition goes smoothly, I figure I won't be too far behind Crusher."

"All of us back within a few months of each other, except for Speed. It's going to be an adjustment. But I'm ready," I said.

"With you there, brother. Looking forward to it myself." I watched Coast's face as he thumbed through each order sheet. If I hadn't, I would have missed the brief change in his expression before it relaxed again. Knowing he wouldn't discuss what brought that on, I didn't bother to ask.

We settled on Chinese food, and I called the order in. Since the place delivered, we took our beers and went into the living room to wait for it to arrive.

"Now that we caught up on the news from home, why don't you fill me in on the woman that left, Jag?"

"Shit, where to start, man," I said, then figured the beginning would be best. How long could it take to cover a few months? Coast listened while I recounted my time with Simone.

"Seriously, brother, your taste in women... Hell, you can pick them." He chuckled, and I wanted to be pissed, but I had no argument or excuse because he was right.

"They haven't all been bad. Most had been the have-fun-while-it-lasted type. And it had been mutual with no strings."

"Uh huh, that's worked over the years for you. Let's see, your car was repainted because the one chick spray painted 'cheating bastard' on both sides while you were in the restaurant with another woman."

"She was the one who said it wasn't working out. After I agreed, I moved on. I can't help it she changed her mind and turned into a stalker. I wouldn't have been so pissed if she'd just painted bastard, it was the cheating part that irked my ass. I don't cheat," I said indignantly, but it didn't bother Coast, he snickered and went on.

"Two slashed bike tires, your gas tank with the words 'I hate you' scratched into it, the nick in your shoulder when the one chick threw the cooking knife at you. Need I continue. Admit it, brother, you draw the strange and crazy."

"Hey, there wasn't anything wrong with Marilee. I really liked her, and I'll even admit that I hated she moved away after graduation."

"Seriously, you have to go back to high school to come up with one? Dude, that is fucking sad."

"It counts!"

Coast shook his head and smirked. "Fine, I'll give you that one. I liked Marilee. She was nice, funny, and smart, even with the crappy foster family she was stuck with."

"See, there is another thing to look forward to about going home. The women around the club and town know the deal," I said.

"True." The doorbell rang right after Coast spoke, and I stood. I looked at him as I walked to the door.

"You know, for the first time, I think I understand why our dads always say they don't need or want ol' ladies."

"I'm not opposed to finding a woman who doesn't play games. A sweet one who doesn't harp and does what I say." I couldn't hold back the laughter at Coast's words.

"Brother, you'd be bored inside a week. At least with the sweet. The game playing, well, I've never been a fan of that shit either."

I pulled the door open and paid for the food. Once I set the containers out on the coffee table, I went and grabbed a couple more beers for us.

It was nice having one of my brothers to hang with for a change. As Coast and I talked more about home and the changes the dads were making within the club, the more at peace I became with my decision. It was time, Black Hawk was definitely where I needed to be.

"To home and one day finding the right woman." I held my bottle out to Coast.

"And until she's found, in the faraway future, plenty to keep the nights from being cold and lonely." Coast tapped his bottle to mine.

As I tipped my bottle and took a drink, my decision to leave the military felt right. Knowing my brothers would be there also just made it that much better.

Chapter One

Jag

"Feels good, doesn't it?" I looked at Coast and Flirt as we placed the finishing touches on the first bikes built under Black Hawk Custom Bikes.

"Fuck yeah, it does," Coast said as he tossed his rag in the bin for the used ones.

"And the best part is, we already have three more orders. Brothers, we can officially consider this a business," Flirt said as he slapped Coast and me on the back.

"We've been a business. You're just saying that because of the money," I said, tossed my rag in the bin, and stood back to look at my handiwork. The chrome reflected the sunrays that filtered through the open bay door of the garage.

"Damn straight. Even after we buy the supplies and parts for the next three orders, we'll end up with a decent profit. All about the numbers, brothers," Flirt said and chuckled when Coast and I groaned.

Every month we go over the books for the club's businesses, and while we griped, Flirt was in his element.

Christ, I'd take a legal brief any day over rows and rows of numbers.

When my cell vibrated, I reached into my back pocket, pulled it out, and looked at the screen, then hit the accept button. "What's up, Boss?" I asked as I held the cell to my ear.

"Hey, VP, Turk and I have the contract for the building we're purchasing to house the cannabis store. Wanted to know if you had the time to take a glance at the papers. We could come to Black Hawk or meet you in town? Whatever works for you."

"I'll come to you. Better yet, meet you at Soft Tails, and we can grab some grub." I went to the workbench and put the tools I used away. There was nothing left to do now but wait for the weekend to roll around and for the buyers to pick up the bikes and pay for the last of their costs. Then on to the next orders.

"That sounds good. But if you have the time, can you meet us at the building beforehand and have a look around? Value another opinion besides mine and Turk's before we sign the paperwork and complete the buy."

"Yeah, no problem. That's doable. See ya in a few, Boss." I touched the disconnect button, slid the cell back in my pocket, and straightened the workbench.

"You heading to town now, Jag?" Coast asked.

"Nah, going to grab a shower first. You two got anything going on? Want to ride?"

"Works for me. I was just going to eat a sandwich at the house after I cleaned up, but a burger and fries and a cold beer sounds a helluva lot better for lunch," Flirt said as he locked the storage room where we kept our additional parts and materials along with the paints.

"The idea of adding the temp control to the storage room was one of Speed's better ideas," I said when Flirt had shut the storage room door.

"Well, true, but don't tell him that, Jag. We'd never hear the end of the shit," Coast said and laughed. He knew, like I did, that Speed wasn't like that. We just enjoyed giving him a hard time. Even more since the high-strung, over the top man with a zero to sixty temper in seconds, had mellowed. Well, at least with Sami and Ally.

"Where is our brother? As a matter of fact, where are Devil and Crusher?" Flirt asked. "I figured they'd want to be here when the last of the touch-ups were done."

"Crusher went with Carly to her last checkup with the physical therapist. If she gets cleared, she'll be back to work at the sheriff's station." I lowered the bay door as I talked and then headed toward the side door. "Speed is with Sami at her appointment with Dr. Minton. And Ghost and Luna tagged along since she has an appointment, too. Last, Dev took Neely to meet with Bailey for her appointment with the pediatrician. Neely, not Bailey." Once we walked out, I locked the door and turned, and Flirt and Coast were grinning. "What?"

"Brother, I'm amazed you felt the need to clarify who was going to the kiddie doctor. I mean, damn, not like we are total morons about kids." Flirt chuckled, then continued. "However, I find it quite amusing on how the mighty have fallen. Don't get me wrong, the women our brothers have chosen are fuckin' awesome, but did either of you ever think when we returned from the military, our lives would change so much in a short amount of time?" Flirt asked as we started walking toward our homes.

"Nope, but with as happy as those fuckers are, I wouldn't mind waking up every morning with a smile on my face," Coast said and kept walking.

"Then lock the doc down, man," Flirt said and earned himself a scowl from Coast.

"I'm not you, Flirt. I refuse to tie her to my damn bed. I much prefer she come to it willingly."

"Don't underestimate the ability an excellent set of ropes has," Flirt said, and I smiled when Coast shook his head and groaned.

"I'm not even going to get started on that shit, Flirt. Fuck me, I try hard not to think about the things I saw when I visited you on leave, and you took me to that club." Coast did a fake shiver, and I cocked my brow.

"Asshole," Flirt said and slapped Coast's shoulder.

"How come I didn't know you and Flirt visited a club?" I asked, and Coast shook his head.

"Because I didn't get any further than one viewing room. Dude, I knew immediately that wasn't for me, and I left Flirt to it. I love being in control, but that was way outside my comfort zone. Hell, before I went in there, I didn't even know I had a comfort zone." Coast shook his head as if to clear the images, and I turned to Flirt.

"You did not let him witness an extreme pain and punishment scene?" Flirt nodded, and Coast's head jerked to me.

"You've been?"

"Yeah, I went while I was in San Diego at Coronado for a joint JAG conference. Some aspects of it interest me, but overall, it really isn't my scene either. But, brother, at least I lasted the evening." I laughed when Coast flipped me off.

"I've explained to both of you, it is a twenty-four/seven lifestyle for some, where the D/s relationship is not just a scene played out in a club. Their lives follow the D/s roles. Besides, your asses didn't have to go. All you had to do was say you weren't interested, and we would have gone somewhere else."

"Don't get your panties twisted, man. Geez, Flirt, talk about dishing it out and not being able to take it." I looked over at Flirt and noticed he had his brows furrowed. "Brother, we weren't putting your preferences down. What's your deal?" As we continued to walk, I glanced at Coast, and he shrugged. He evidently didn't know what brought on the sudden change in Flirt.

"I don't need, nor want the twenty-four/seven lifestyle, but yeah, I enjoy controlling what is going on, and the rush I get as my partner turns over her pleasure to me because I've taken her into subspace where she trusts that I'll give her exactly what she wants and needs. I don't have the desire to lead a woman around on a leash or have her sit at my feet to feel a connection. What I want, though, is a strong woman. One who can manage anything thrown her way but realizes she doesn't have to when she's with me. She'll know I'll take care of her—mentally, physically, and sexually."

Coast and I watched Flirt as he spoke, and I wondered if Coast noticed the wistful look in Flirt's eyes as he told us exactly what he was looking for in a woman. I also knew when Flirt found the one who fit what he needed, he wouldn't avoid her. She'd be locked down before she even knew what had happened to her.

"That's you, brother. And I hope you find everything you want in a woman. But I can't see the doc allowing anyone to control her, and frankly, I don't need her to let me. What I need her to do is stop avoiding me long enough to show her I'm the one for her. Every single time I've gotten close to her since we came back from San Diego, she turns and runs in the opposite direction. One of these days, there isn't going to be a place for her to escape. I'm out of patience," Coast said as we stopped in the middle of the road between our places.

"Uh... patience? I don't think I've ever heard your name, and that word used in the same sentence," I said, then dodged the punch Coast aimed at me.

"Joke all you want. Noticed you've been surly lately. Wouldn't have anything to do with River, would it?" I sneered at Coast, who laughed since my actions didn't faze him.

"Don't like it when you're the one under the microscope, huh, VP?" Flirt said. Seemed he was over his little snit as he chuckled right along with Coast.

Assholes.

"What the fuck ever. I'm going to take a shower," I said and turned toward my place.

"Meet ya out here in twenty, so don't take too long in that shower!" I kept walking, threw my arm in the air and flipped Coast off. When would I learn not to talk to the bastards about shit?

"Fuck the both of you. It might be time to find some new friends!" I yelled without turning around, but their laughter followed me as I closed the front door.

I stripped as soon as I hit my bedroom and headed to the bathroom, where I turned the shower on.

River was going to have to be dealt with. She could throw all the attitude she wanted—I needed to know if something was there between us or not. Thanks to Luna and her voiced opinion of sexual tension, which was made from witnessing River and me in front of Yoga Sensual the day she nearly ran over me coming out the door.

So what if I'd had a couple of dreams about the woman. It wasn't like my brothers had been around the woman any more than I had. Ghost fixed a fucking window for her. Big damn deal. And how the fuck was I supposed to get to know someone who sneered every time I was around them? It mattered not what her ass looked like in yoga pants, jeans, or a tight skirt and heels.

I checked the temperature of the spray and stepped into the shower with the redhead on my mind. If I was honest, she'd been on my mind a lot since that first day in the parking lot of the courthouse. The hot water ran down my body and just like any other time I thought of River, my shaft hardened. Screw it, the guys could wait for all I cared. I ran my hand down, then wrapped it around my straining cock and closed my eyes.

"Something has to give," I whispered. I only wished I knew the outcome once it did. The damn woman had me touching myself like a green, fresh-faced teen who hadn't been close to a woman, never mind sinking into the warmth of one.

With the hot water blasting me, I moved my hand up and down. Every slide earned a curse. If I kept thinking about her, I was going to need to buy a brace for my wrist and invest in a shit ton of lotion.

River's face surfaced behind my eyelids. What was wrong with me? I'd stayed away from any woman in town who would want more than to scratch an itch. The ones who hung around the club knew the deal, which was mainly the strippers at Soft Tails. Since my brothers had been dropping like flies, the parties were far and in between now. Unless it had to do with a family celebration.

Whatever the reason, my problem wasn't going to be fixed in the shower. I focused on River's face and picked up speed as I squeezed and twisted my hand. It didn't take long to bring myself to the brink when I pictured River on her knees with her lips surrounding me, and my hands full of her red hair.

"Fuck!" I screamed as my release splashed against the shower tile. Spent, I leaned my forehead against the wall and squeezed my eyes tighter.

Acknowledging Luna's theory, I wondered what River Ramey would have to say. If past encounters with her were anything to go by, I was pretty sure the woman would mock me.

I washed, then stepped out of the shower. When I looked in the mirror, I grinned. Could be time to be proactive in the situation. Some good friction might just melt the layer of ice she wore like a suit of armor.

If I walked through the flames in hell, maybe we would both get what we wanted. Getting River to ask for it would make it even better.

As I finished drying off and dressed, the smile left my face. I hadn't had the best history with the opposite sex, and with that knowledge, I knew the woman would drive me to the brink of insanity before she succumbed.

It also hadn't slipped past me that she pushed buttons I didn't even know I had. With keys in hand, I walked out my door and headed toward my bike. Maybe it was time I pushed a few buttons myself.

Chapter Two

River

Looking in the mirror, I adjusted the straps of my bra under the black tank top and rotated around to see how my jeans fit.

"New place, new job, and a new me," I repeated the same words every day since I arrived in Shades Valley. I picked up the brush and worked it through my thick, red hair until I had the wavy strands in my hand, then twisted them and snapped the sizeable black clip into the wild mess. When I let go, my hair was piled on my head in a makeshift ponytail that actually looked good on me. It had been a long time since I felt comfortable in my skin—if ever. Funny how it only had taken moving across the country to achieve it.

With one last look, I headed out into the bedroom and inwardly groaned at the clothes tossed on my bed. Yeah, I might have changed a few times before I settled on my current outfit. If Thomas saw me now, he'd voice his disapproval for sure.

"River, your outfit does not reflect that of a partner's wife." Never mind, he wasn't a partner yet, only the son of one who was promised the advancement and votes of the other two partners if he showed his father he was a committed family man. And what better way to tip the scales in his favor than marry the stepdaughter of one of the other partners.

Yeah, that worked out well.

Thomas was my past, and I needed to keep him there. He no longer had any say in what I wanted or needed. I'd let him have too much power over me when we were together. But no more. I'd made the break and now controlled my life for the first time. The thought of that made me smile as I sat on the edge of the bed and pulled on my boots.

With my boots on, I left the bedroom, went downstairs, grabbed my purse and jacket, then headed out the door. I'd spent enough time getting my house unpacked and livable. I even had everything filled out and ready to begin my job, though I still had a bit before I would officially start. All that was left was the invention of the new me. Not so much inventing—more like finding my true self.

The woman I was meant to be had to be buried in there somewhere, right?

I locked the door and started toward my car. The small Mercedes stood out on the street where I lived, and it would be the next thing I changed and the last thing I owned from my old life. That was how I'd categorized things—old and new.

"Hi!"

I turned toward the voice and smiled at the little girl who walked toward me from the neighbor's yard. Her black hair was pulled up in a ponytail that swung with each step as she moved closer. I'd seen her a few times around town, along with her coming and going from Sue Mayson's place. She was the daughter of the woman I purchased the house from, Sami Borelli, though the little girl looked nothing like her mother. She was, however, the feminine version of her dad, Kane, one of the bikers who dropped her off or picked her from Sue's place. That thought immediately brought the man who haunted my thoughts since the first time I'd laid eyes on him. The same man I seemed to always run into, literally. Dominic Amara. Jag to his biker buddies.

Each time his presence sent me spiraling into a woman I had no clue existed inside me. He had dark blue eyes that were in contrast with his dark brown hair and olive skin tone. And when the man focused those sapphire globes on me, my blood warmed, and my insides tingled. Those thoughts of him needed to be curbed pronto. If not for my sake, then for the little girl's.

"Hi yourself."

She stopped right in front of me and looked up through eyes that seemed much older than she appeared.

"Do you live here now?"

"Yes, I do. What's your name, sweetie?"

"Ally. I lived here before my daddy came and found my momma and me. Now we live with him. Aunt Carly was supposed to live here, but Uncle Crusher made her move in with him." My lips twitched. She was too cute and talkative. "Is somebody gonna make you live with them, too?"

"Umm... I don't think so."

"Got kids?"

"Sorry, no. I..." I cut myself off before I explained further. The little girl didn't need to hear my troubles.

"Why? Don't you like kids?" Ally asked and frowned at me.

"I like them very much. It's, well... I don't have a husband," I added at the end. It was the easiest way as an explanation.

"You don't need one to get a kid. Uncle Dev brought one home for Aunt Bailey. Neely's not a baby, though, she's three and my friend. Since Aunt Bailey didn't have her like my momma had me, Neely's their sister. My momma's gonna have me a sister because I don't want a brother. And she don't have a husband either. She's only got my daddy. But my papa told him she needs to have a husband before his next grandbaby gets here."

I bit the inside of my cheek to keep from chuckling. I imagined Ally kept her parents on their toes. Listening to her gave me some idea of what I would face when I started teaching at the elementary school.

"Well, I'm sure your momma will do the best she can to give you a sister, but sometimes little boys show up despite it all."

"I think my daddy wants a boy."

"Oh, sweetie, I'm sure he will be happy no matter if it is a boy or a girl."

"I don't think so. I heard him tell my uncles our house needs more tetesron. What's that mean?" Ally wrinkled her nose as she asked, and I had to work hard not to smile. No way did I want the little girl to think I was laughing at her.

"Well... Um... I think he meant if your momma has a boy, then it would even the numbers in your home. You know, two boys and two girls?" I explained and watched her eyebrows scrunch together, making me wonder if she understood.

"'K, but I think it's because boys pee standing up."

Out of the mouth of babes. Maybe I wasn't going to be a good teacher because the chuckle escaped me at her words and, by the serious look on her face, she didn't think it was humorous.

"Sorry, sweetie, I didn't mean to laugh. But why would you think that?"

"Because Benji says boys are better than girls cause they gotsa penis and can pee standing up."

I had no clue who Benji was, and I wasn't sure I wanted to know. However, I hoped he wasn't going to be in my class.

Before I could dig a deeper hole by asking who Benji was, the sound of a vehicle coming up the street saved me. Ally and I both turned and watched as the truck pulled into Sue's driveway.

"Crap," Ally muttered, and I looked down at her. When she looked up at me, she grinned sheepishly.

"Ally! Does Sue know you're out here?" Ally's dad asked as he slid out of the driver's side of the truck and walked around to the other side, opened the door, and helped Sami out. I'd met Sami and Carly briefly when they came by the house because Sami wanted to apologize for not being the one to drop the house keys and paperwork off to me.

"Gotta go!" Ally yelled and started across the yard, then stopped and looked over her shoulder at me. "If you want a baby, I gotta lot of uncles who could give you one!"

"Um... Well... I'll have to think about that," I said and smiled. Ally smiled back, then took off at a run.

"Am I gettin' a sister?!" Ally yelled as she continued across the lawn toward her parents.

When she reached her dad, he swooped her up until she sat on his shoulders. Ally's laughter filled the air as I watched the interaction with the family. Sami smiled at Ally, then glanced over at me and said something to Ally that I couldn't hear.

Feeling like an interloper at their private moment, I stuck my key into the lock on my car door and pulled it open. Before I could get into the driver's side, Sami's voice stopped me.

"River, good to see you. How's everything going? Are you finally settled in?" Sami asked, as I glanced up.

"Good to see you, too. Yes, I finally have everything unpacked and put away," I answered as Sami reached my car.

Sami rubbed a hand over her stomach, and I followed the motion. Sadness tried to push through, but I refused to let it. Not having a child with Thomas had only been one bleep in the issues of our marriage. I had wanted something to love that would love me back, and he needed an heir to advance his career. Neither of us got what we wanted, which was probably for the best, since the reasons for wanting a child weren't the right ones. But even that knowledge hadn't helped as each month passed and I received negative results. I felt more inadequate as a woman, and he grew more bitter, more hateful, and placed the blame on me. But his last betrayal and the knowledge of it left me empty and was the last straw to break a marriage that probably shouldn't have taken place. Sami spoke, and it pulled me out of those spiraling thoughts.

"That's great. I hope Ally wasn't bothering you?" The way Sami's eyes lit when she mentioned her daughter showed the love she had for the little girl. It was also sad that I couldn't remember seeing anything remotely close to that look in my mother's eyes.

Yeah, one more item for me to analyze later when I was alone.

"Not at all. She is so cute and funny. I bet she's a handful. How old is she?"

"Five, going on twenty." Sami laughed. "And you are being kind. The girl is nosey, and she doesn't understand boundaries. Nor does she have any type of filter on what comes out of her mouth."

"You don't find many her age who do. Will she be in kindergarten this year?" I asked. Small talk I could do. It was the whole making of new friends that was foreign to me. One more thing to change.

"Yes. She recently finished preschool and is out for the summer. But she is looking forward to being in *real* school, as she calls it." Sami rolled her eyes, and I chuckled.

"Well, I'm glad she is looking forward to it. It will make my job a lot easier. If she is in my class. I'm the new kindergarten teacher at Shades Valley Elementary. I'm replacing Mrs. Staples, who retired at the end of this school year. At least that was what I was told when they hired me." I smiled, and Sami nodded.

"Yes, when we received the letter about pre-registration for Ally, it mentioned her retirement, along with the hiring of her replacement. They didn't give a name, though. So, congratulations."

"Thank you. I'm looking forward to finally using my teaching degree."

"I'm surprised you would move from the east coast to the west coast for a teaching position. Were there not any openings at schools in your area in Connecticut? That's where you are from, right? I can't imagine moving across the country. You must have—" Sami abruptly stopped mid-sentence, then grinned sheepishly as her daughter had previously done. "God, River, I'm so sorry. Ignore everything I said. Seems my daughter comes by her nosiness honestly. Either that or this baby is draining my brain cells from the part of my brain that controls manners and my mouth." Sami grinned, rubbed her stomach once more, and shook her head.

"You're fine. I didn't take it like that. But to answer, I just needed a change in scenery." The more we talked, the more relaxed I became. Everyone I'd met and spoken with since I moved to town had been friendly. Except for one, which I refused to focus on.

"It's so nice getting to talk with you more, River. The time Carly and I stopped by, I was still fighting morning sickness. Thankfully, that seems to be over."

"Glad you're feeling better. Do you know what you're having?"

"Ah, see, now I know Ally talked your ears off. She has been relentless in having a sister. But she isn't getting her wish. I had a sonogram this morning at Dr. Minton's office, and the baby was more than cooperative, so definitely having a boy."

"Congrats to you and Kane!"

Sami nodded. "Thanks. Though I wouldn't have cared either way, it would have made it convenient since I have all the baby girl things from Ally." Sami smiled. "With the cost of baby items, it would have been nice not to have to purchase everything over again. However, with this one, I won't have to fight about clothing when he gets older. I never got to have the mother's experience of dressing her daughter in all the cute girly things. Once Ally turned old enough to complain, it wasn't worth the fight. I couldn't get the girl in a dress. Now it's jeans, biker boots, and t-shirts. Kane will buy everything in sight for a boy and do it without complaint. Don't get me wrong, he would be just as happy to be getting another daughter. He was more worried that with another girl he wouldn't have any hair left." Sami chuckled.

"So, it isn't because boys can pee standing up?" I asked teasingly, then laughed when Sami's eyes went wide.

"Oh my God, that girl. I don't know what I'm going to do with her. I'm going to go ahead and apologize right now for anything else she said."

"No worries, we'll call it even if you tell me the kid named Benji is older and there isn't any chance he'll be in my class." I lifted a brow, and Sami laughed.

"Oh, River, I should already set up monthly or weekly visits with you," Sami said, and continued to laugh.

"Hmm... and I was looking so forward to teaching. I'm thinking I may have bitten off more than I can chew." I chuckled along with Sami. I couldn't remember ever talking with someone so easily. I had a feeling it was Sami. She was sweet and made it easy to relax around her.

"Better yet, I'll send Kane and his brothers to the meetings since it's their fault Ally is like she is. They spoil her unashamedly. But in their defense, she has them wrapped around her fingers and takes full advantage of the fact that not one of them can say no to her."

"Hey, at least your life isn't boring, right?"

"Isn't that the truth," Sami answered, as the sound of another vehicle had us both turning. We watched together as it pulled to the curb in front of Sue's house.

When the driver's door opened, a dark-haired man with a goatee got out, then leaned into the backseat. As he stood from inside the car, he held a little girl with hair a few shades lighter than his. We continued to watch as the small child said something that made the man smile, then he placed his large hand over her face and rubbed down. The little girl laughed, leaned in, and blew a raspberry on his cheek, which had the man making gagging noises, and the little girl laughing harder.

"He is so good with her. He's going to make a terrific dad." When I glanced at Sami, I must have had a questioning look on my face because she chuckled and explained, "That's Devil, and the little girl is Neely, his sister."

"Oh, Ally mentioned Neely," I said, and left out the rest Ally had shared with me.

"Yes, Ally and Neely hit it off right from the start when Devil brought her home."

I wanted to ask Sami more, but it wasn't my place. Whatever brought the siblings together wasn't as important as how happy they looked with each other.

"Hey, hot momma, your old man in the house? You know I've got to congratulate him on creating a baby with a stem," the man said as he walked toward us. His eyes gleamed with mischief and, between that and the smirk he wore, I didn't need an explanation on why he was called Devil.

"You're an as... butt, Dev."

"Nice catch, Sami. And yep, Bailey tells me frequently."

Sami snorted. "Kane's checking to make sure Sue doesn't mind watching Ally a little longer while we all go out to lunch," Sami said, and rolled her eyes before she looked at me. "River, this is Lance "Devil" Cummings, and the sweetheart in his arms is Neely. Dev, this is River Ramey."

"Hey, River, nice to meet you. I've seen you around town and leaving the yoga place a couple times, but never got the chance to introduce myself," he said, looked me over, and then when his eyes met mine, a slow smile spread across his face.

"Nice to meet you, too. And you, Neely," I added, and the little girl smiled and laid her head on Devil's shoulder. His perusal made me feel as if he knew something I didn't.

"I would love to stand outside and talk to two beautiful women, but this one is ready for a nap," he said and ran his hand over Neely's hair. "Ready to go see Sue and Ally, squirt?" Once Neely nodded, Devil turned to Sami. "Are Luna and Ghost going to join us, or are they heading back to Black Hawk?"

"They'll meet us there. They were swinging by the Harley store first. Luna was complaining she needed a few things because some of her clothes were getting a little snug," Sami said, then turned to me. "I forgot you already know Luna and Ghost. You've met Jag, too, right? Plus, you know Carly and me, and now Dev. So you've got a good start on meeting some of the club. Why don't you join us for lunch and you'll get a chance to officially meet Kane and a few others from the club? And there are always quite a few locals who come through for lunch."

"While you ladies work on a plan, I'm going to take Neely to the house before she goes completely out. See you soon, River," Devil said, winked, then turned toward Sue's before I could answer.

"Hold up, Dev, I'll walk with you," Sami said, and Devil stopped. "What do you say, River, join us for lunch? Perry, the cook at Soft Tails, makes the best fried chicken in town and you can't beat his burger and fries either. Unless you don't like fresh and prefer the processed stuff the clown tries to push off as beef."

"You're having lunch at a strip club?" I flinched as the question came out of my mouth before I could pull it back. And I was appalled, more than surprised, that my tone of voice sounded like my mother's.

As I worked on an apology, Devil's laughter stopped me and when Sami spoke her lips twitched, "Yes, Soft Tails is a strip club and now a bar. Recently, the club renovated the front to just a bar with food. The strip club will be in the back once they get the addition finished. Since the girls are waiting for the new place to open, a few are filling in as waitresses in the bar. And the others took time off to go on vacation or visit family and friends."

"Sorry, it caught me off guard, and I really didn't mean to sound like a prude."

"Never been in a strip club, huh?" Devil asked with humor in his voice. It was hard not to feel relaxed around him between how he treated his sister and his easygoing, flirty personality. Enough so, I dropped some of the protective shield I had built over the years.

"Not since I stopped dancing to become a kindergarten teacher," I said, and there was a moment of silence while Devil blankly looked at me until Sami chuckled.

"I wish I had gotten a pic of your face, Dev. Thank you, River. I don't think I've ever seen him speechless."

"Well, shit," Devil said and grinned.

"Well shit," Neely repeated, and both Sami and I cocked a brow at Devil.

"Shush, don't repeat that, okay?" Devil's reprimand had Neely snuggling her face more into his neck. With his free hand, he rubbed over her hair and down until it rested on her back and he patted. "You want us to get in trouble if Bailey hears you say that?" Neely shook her head, then Devil said, "That's right, little sis, we got each other's back."

I wondered if there was anyone who dared to tell the big bikers that they evidently turned into softies with the little girls in their lives.

"No," Sami said, and laughed.

"Oh, damn... um, did I say that out loud?" It seemed I was more relaxed around these people than I first thought.

"Oh, damn." When the words left Neely's mouth, I palmed my face.

Devil chuckled. "Uh yeah, now you have to come to lunch. You'll need to explain to Bailey that you're to blame before that gets repeated in the house."

"What? Neely agreed not to repeat what you said. You won't say that naughty word, will you, sweetie?" Neely's face turned to me, and she blinked sleepily, then her lips curved up. In that second, was the resemblance to her brother that I hadn't noticed before.

"Hey, you can't horn in on my deal. Besides, you need to meet Bailey, anyway. Not to mention, I could use the entertainment." Sami smacked Devil's arm, and he grinned down at her. "What?"

"Behave," was Sami's reply to Devil. And once again, I felt as if I missed something between the two.

"Geez, pregnancy is making you a little mean, Sami. Hope it isn't what I've got to look forward to with Bay." Dev cringed, and I laughed when Sami rolled her eyes and shook her head.

"I was on my way out to run a couple of errands, so I guess I could meet you there. Is that alright?" If I was going to live here and be a part of the community, I needed to make an effort.

"That's great. You know where the club is, right?" I nodded, and then Sami said, "Will twelve work for you?"

I looked at my watch. "Yes, that will be perfect."

"Okay, see you then," Sami said, and linked her arm with Devil's, and they headed toward Sue's house while I got in my car, backed out of my driveway, and drove down the street.

I knew the men and women were part of the Black Hawk MC. My dad had told me about the local motorcycle club when I had made the move. He'd even mentioned the house Sami had for sale when I told him I had no plans to live with him. Thankfully, he hadn't argued with me because I would have given in to keep the peace, just like I'd done my whole life with my mother. Instead, my dad had done what he always had over the years; listened without judgment and supported my decisions, even if he hadn't agreed with them. He had been and continued to be the one person in my life to love me unconditionally.

The parking lot at the post office only held a few cars as I pulled in and parked. I grinned as I got out of the car and thought of what my dad would say when I told him I was going to a strip club to meet some bikers and their women. Then I frowned because my thoughts changed to the rude one I'd already encountered more than once. Hopefully, he wouldn't be there.

I walked in and surveyed the lobby, then stepped behind an elderly woman who already stood at the counter. As I waited, I decided I wasn't going to let one person keep me from meeting a wonderful group of people, no matter how attractive he was or the way he smelled each time I was around him—all man. A real man, not the expensive cologne wearing type whose hands were softer than a baby's bottom. His weren't. They were large, and the day he ran into me at Yoga Sensual, I felt the roughness when he accidentally touched me as he helped to pick the things up that fell out of my bag... and if I closed my eyes; I knew I would feel them on my skin as they traveled over my body. No doubt the man had plenty of experience with women, and I wondered what it would be like to have the undivided attention on my body from a man like that.

"That has to be someone special you're thinking of." I jumped at the voice and looked up and saw the elderly lady had finished with her business and the woman behind the counter grinned at me.

"Excuse me?" I blinked and stepped forward.

"Oh, hon, a woman with a dreamy look and flushed face, who doesn't answer when called, no doubt a man is involved." The woman winked, and I felt mortified, as though she knew exactly what had been going on in my head. Manners were the only thing that kept me from turning around and walking out.

"No man, I'm afraid." I forced a chuckle. "Just running through everything I need to get done today."

The woman smiled, and I knew she hadn't bought the lame excuse, but I was grateful she hadn't called me out on it. I bought my stamps, mailed my bills, and was on my way to my next stop. And when the man tried to push forward in my head again, I shut him out. He had his time taking up space there, and I wasn't interested in his continued appearance.

When I got back in my car, and the voice in my head chanted, *lair, lair, pants on fire*, I told her to shut up, pulled out of the parking lot and totally ignored the mocking laughter as it echoed in my mind.

By the time I made it to my next stop, I walked into the building and headed straight for the office without speaking to anyone. I threw the door open and asked, "Are people who live in this town more apt to suffer bouts with their sanity?"

"Not to my knowledge. Why don't you close the door and have a seat, sweetheart? Then you can tell me what's got you so flustered." The sheriff leaned back in his chair, and I sat and began my rant. And if I hadn't been acting neurotic at that moment, I might have noticed his eyes change from sparkling with humor to frowning with concern.

Chapter Three

Jag

"This building is in great shape. Not a lot of work to do to bring it up to code. Price is reasonable. The biggest expense is the security system you want to put in," I said as I walked out the back door of the building Boss and Turk were buying.

"Might want to replace this outer door, though. Replace the hollow steel with a solid one and add a door bar. Not that someone would be stupid enough to hit a club business, but no sense enticing them with easy access," Coast said as he looked over the door and its framework.

"Yeah, that was what we thought, too. Turk and I also discussed changing out the plate-glass windows in the front or at the very least adding steel bars." I followed Boss around the side to the front with the others.

"I'd go with the ballistic glass. Security with a clear view instead of the bars," Flirt said, and everyone nodded in agreement.

As we stood on the sidewalk and discussed a few other changes and upgrades, the door to the bakery next door opened and Romeo, Flirt's dad, walked out with Claire.

"Sheriff's going to ticket you boys for loitering," Romeo said as they walked up to join us. I hadn't missed the proprietary gesture of Romeo's hand at the small of Claire's back and neither had Flirt.

"Maybe Boss and Turk should look at a different area for the store. Seems this part of town has a few unsavory characters lurking around," Flirt said, and his dad laughed.

"Now, is that any way to talk about Claire? She's been in business around here for a long time." Romeo leaned down and kissed the top of Claire's head, and a faint blush rose on her cheeks. I lifted a brow at the suggestion the move made. Seemed a lot of changes were happening in the club these days.

"So, not just interested in the sweets sold in the bakery, huh?" I groaned at Flirt's attempt at subtlety while Coast, Boss, and Turk coughed to cover up their laughter.

"Good grief, I've never known one of you boys to beat around the bush about anything. Ask what's on your mind, Flirt. Better yet, let me answer it and get everything out in the open. I'm seeing Michael and guess what? We are attracted to each other and don't you," Claire pointed at me, "act all damn surprised because I know you've seen me leaving a few mornings from Black Hawk. That's what is wrong with young people, you think to dang much instead of trusting your feelings. Life is short, don't ever put off things or you might run out of time. That's one thing I learned the hard way. When I got sick, I promised myself then if I came through the ordeal, I wouldn't put off doing or even saying whatever I want."

Claire turned and walked back to the bakery while I and the others stood there and stared after her. No one said anything until the door closed behind her.

"Well, so much for not wanting to embarrass her by bringing up that I've seen her on more than one occasion leaving the compound early in the morning," I said, and grinned at Romeo.

"Yeah, she mentioned it to me several times. The first time you saw her, she expected to have Bailey stopping in the bakery that day. She has stopped by her mother's house while I've been there, but she doesn't say or ask anything."

"Maybe she thinks if something serious is going on that you and her mother will have the decency to tell her." Romeo glanced at Flirt and his brows lowered. Coast and I moved closer in case we needed to act fast to keep father and son from each other.

"I don't get in your personal business, and I expect the same respect. No, I demand the fucking respect. So, you better say now if you and I are going to have a problem, son." Romeo stepped closer, and this time, Boss and Turk moved to a better position to help Coast and me if the situation turned to the worst.

"Hell no, I'll always have respect for you and will stand behind you, right or wrong, but..." Flirt cut off and chuckled, which relaxed everyone, "if you hurt that woman, it will be because of that respect I won't let Bailey kill you; however, I will let her take some hide off your ass, then I'll take you to the hospital." We laughed with Flirt, and so did Romeo.

"Well, then it's a damn good thing I don't plan to hurt her, but..." Romeo said as he mimicked Flirt before he went on. "I do plan to make her my ol' lady, and that includes marrying her. So, if Bailey feels the need to tear off some hide, I'll let her. Won't change nothing. I'm going to marry her mama, whether she or anyone else thinks I'm not good enough for her." A few minutes of quiet went by before anyone of us responded to Romeo's declaration.

"Sonofabitch, I'm not eating or drinking another damn thing at the clubhouse. Motherfuckers are dropping like flies." I looked over at Turk, and he shook his head.

"I'm with you, Turk," Boss said, and the brothers bumped knuckles.

"Since I told you my plan before I've even asked Claire, let me tell you that if it gets back to her before I get the chance, I'll tear some goddamned hide off some asses myself." Romeo looked at each of us and lifted a brow.

After we agreed to keep our mouths shut, he mentioned the reason for coming out to talk with us.

"I wanted to see if Boss and Turk would add in a couple surveillance cameras that point toward Claire's shop. Figured the added security for her place couldn't hurt with the cannabis store next to it."

"Don't see a problem. I can add it on to our order, then mention it at the next club meeting." Boss looked at me after he answered Romeo.

"Yeah, do that, Boss. Romeo, you know we're at least going to inform Crusher, Devil, and Speed on why. Right?"

"I know, Jag, and appreciate it, but we know what's going to happen if the women get wind of the reason. I was hoping the cameras could be added and I would personally pay the extra cost."

"Are you suggesting that our brothers' ol' ladies can't keep their mouths closed?" I asked and could not keep my lips from twitching.

"Not saying they would blab all over town. Now, amongst themselves, hell yes, which is exactly what I want to avoid. I don't want everyone in the club knowing before Claire," Romeo said, and glanced over his shoulder as if to make sure Claire hadn't snuck up on him from the bakery.

"Afraid she might not want to lock herself to your old ass and say no?" Flirt asked, and his dad glared.

"Always got to be a smartass. And just because I'm getting a little gray around the edges, don't mean I can't hold my own in taking you down a notch."

"Yeah, keep thinking that, old man. Your delusional thinking will keep you young," Flirt said and slapped Romeo's back.

"You know, we could pass off the extra cameras as looking out for Bailey's mom," Coast suggested, then looked at me and cocked a brow.

"I don't see a problem with it. The women won't know the real reason until Romeo has his woman locked down. Ya know, club business and all," I said, and Boss and Turk shook their heads.

"What?" I asked.

"First off, no disrespect intended, VP. But the women in the club don't miss much. Hell, they probably know more about what goes on than any of us do."

"You could be right, Boss." I couldn't argue with Boss's assessment, and neither could the others.

We went back to the discussion of security equipment and where we thought the best placement for the outside surveillance would be.

"Ya know, with the store going here, Claire's bakery could see more traffic than it already does," Flirt said, and the rest of us stared at him until what he referred to registered.

"Get their medicinal products here, then stop at Claire's and pick up sweets for the munchies later," I said and chuckled.

"Well, shit. Maybe we should attach one of those awnings on the front and add a few tables with chairs, then they don't have to wait until they're home to have a toke and enjoy," Turk said seriously, then turned to look over the front of the building.

The thought really had merit, and I tried to picture if it would work out.

"As entertaining as this is, I think I'll leave you to it and go take my woman to lunch," Romeo announced.

"You and Claire heading to Soft Tails to eat?" I asked as I stopped looking at the building and turned toward Romeo.

"Nah, not today. We're meeting Cruz at Thelma's diner." I didn't miss Romeo's eyes when they shifted to Coast and back. *Interesting.* Seemed lately the dads had been up to more than fishing and riding their bikes. Also made me wonder if I'd missed anything with my old man.

"Alright, tell Thelma we said hey and try to stay out of trouble," I said, and Romeo grinned.

As he turned toward the bakery and walked away, he spoke over his shoulder, "Not a chance in hell. It's you boys' responsibility to keep us in line. Good luck with that, too." Romeo's laughter was cut off as the bakery door closed behind him.

"Damn, I'm having a beer with lunch while I go over the paperwork for this building. Let's lock this place up and head to Soft Tails. Since we pass the sheriff's station on our way, I need to stop there."

"Why? Got a ticket that needs to be paid?" Coast asked.

"No. Sheriff asked me to look over some documents for him." I shrugged.

"Damn, you are in demand, Jag. You might want a building of your own to hang a shingle out," Flirt said, and I flipped him off.

"As if I've got the time between the bike shop and club shit. Besides, the sheriff has always treated the club fair. It's the least I can do for him."

Everyone agreed with me, and after the building was locked up tight, we mounted our bikes and headed down the main road through town.

As we grew closer to the station house, a man and woman embraced on the sidewalk and I grinned when I recognized the man was Sheriff Lance. The woman he had his arms wrapped around had her back toward the road, which wasn't a bad thing in my eyes. The jeans she wore hugged her ass, and that alone was drool-worthy on the woman. The sheriff being a lucky man went through my head as we reached where the couple stood and pulled into the parking lot that was on the side of the station. The noise from our pipes had the couple breaking apart, but the sheriff left an arm around the woman's waist as they turned and watched us pull in.

After we parked, I swung my leg over my bike and dismounted while the others stayed on their bikes to wait. When I turned toward the pair and got my first good look at the woman, my appetite left. My blood pressure surely was on the rise since a red haze moved over my eyes as I focused on the woman's face. My teeth ground with every step I took, and there was no need for a mirror to show me the veins in my neck pulsed. I felt them, and the ones in my temples because they throbbed in a synchronized beat.

"How's it going, Dom?" Sheriff Lance asked as I approached, but I hadn't taken my eyes off the woman beside him with her chin stuck out as she glared at me.

"Good. Was in town so I thought I'd stop by and grab the papers you wanted me to look over. You seem busy, though, so if you need me to grab them later, that's cool," the tone of my voice as I spoke was harsh to my own ears.

"Nah, I'm not busy, Dom. I didn't expect you to come by and pick up the paperwork. You're doing me a favor. I would have brought them out to the club. But I want to know why you are staring at River. You got a problem with my—"

"You don't need to take up for me. I can handle the man's rudeness. We've had a couple of incidents. Nothing to worry about." River glared back at me, and I sneered. Incidents was a nice way of putting it.

"Incidents, my ass. That day, if I'd been one second sooner to that parking spot, I wouldn't be standing here. And if that wasn't bad enough, the next time I see you, you try to take me out on the sidewalk," I gritted out through my teeth.

My morning pep talk about the woman in front of me went to the wayside. And Luna was way off base in her take on River and me. No one was going to get second-degree burns from the heat between us. They were more likely to get blown up.

"Exaggerate much," River said and rolled her eyes.

"No, but I wonder how you walk with the stick up your as—"

"Okay, I think that's enough," the sheriff cut me off while he moved the arm around River's waist to grab her forearm when she took a step toward me.

The sheriff shook his head and grinned when River looked up at him.

"I think it's time for you to be on your way. Drive safe, okay, baby?" The sheriff chuckled when River glared at him. Then he leaned down and kissed her forehead.

"Fine. Whatever. Don't forget dinner tonight. You're still coming, right?" River asked as she stepped away when the sheriff let her arm loose.

"Wouldn't miss it," Sheriff Lance answered and waved his arm toward the front entrance to the station. "If you'll follow me to my office, Dom, I'll grab those papers for you."

"No problem." I gave a last sneer at River, then turned away.

"I'll have everything you like ready and waiting," River yelled. When I glanced over my shoulder, she stepped toward the parking lot and headed to her car. I was surprised I hadn't noticed the little silver Mercedes when we pulled in.

"Make sure you don't run over my brothers when you pull out," I yelled and continued to follow the sheriff.

"Thanks! And why don't you try not to be an insolent asshole?" River was in her car before I had the chance to respond to her parting shot. My disposition went further into the toilet when I noticed my brothers sat on their bikes grinning.

"Fuck everybody," I mumbled, then flipped my brothers off as I walked into the station. The sheriff was already in his office, and I nodded to Shirley as I passed her desk and walked through the doorway.

"Appreciate you taking time to look at this for me. I haven't changed anything in years, and I'm sure there's stuff that needs adjusted, increased, or added. My will is in there, a few stocks, my personal insurance policy and 401K. Also, my pension information and the insurance policy included with my job that I'll have an option of keeping whenever I leave my position. If you find anything I'm missing or should have in place, please give me the suggestions. I want to make sure River is taken care of if anything happens to me."

"Why would you want to do this for a woman who's been with you, for what? A couple months?"

Will Lance was a smart man and a friend to the club. No way would I let some young woman take everything the man had worked for.

"Because she's mine, Dom, and I love her. That's why most men do these things. River moved here to be close to me after her divorce, and I won't let anything, or anyone, hurt her again. I know about the run-ins the two of you have had. She told me about them. I think you've misunderstood what is between her and I. And what you witnessed in front of the station probably didn't help. I don't know why she stopped me from telling you outside," the sheriff said, and shook his head. For what, I had no clue. There was no need for an explanation in my book. Anyone driving by that saw them together wouldn't need one.

"No need for you to explain. I think I fully understand. But you asked me to look at these papers for you, so it technically makes me your counsel, and being that, I'm required to give the best advice I have to offer. Hold off on any changes for now. I understand you think you have feelings for her, but do you know if she has the same feelings for you?"

"Dom, I'd really like to explain what is between River and me. You've got the wrong impres—"

"Nope, we're good, Will. Your personal life is just that. You're a good friend to everyone at Black Hawk, and I wouldn't feel like I was doing my job if I didn't at least try to get you to change your mind. Let me give these a once over, then you and I can sit down and talk after. If you still feel the same, well, I'll do what my client asks of me within the legal system. However, I can set it up where you won't lose anything that you've worked for if the relationship goes south." I took the manila envelope he pulled out of his desk and had held out to me.

"Alright, we'll talk after you read through the papers, son. I think once you go through them, you'll get a clearer picture," Sheriff Lance said, then chuckled when I frowned.

"How can you find humor when some young woman, recently divorced no less, and probably took the ex for a pretty fucking penny, has now set her sights on you? Don't get me wrong, with a body like hers, a dying man would react if she walked in. But shit, Will. Enjoy it for a while. There's no reason to let a piece of as—" I stopped my rant when

Will's hand went up. As he looked at me, his lips went tight, and his eyes flashed with anger.

"You're going to want to stop right there and mind what you say about River. I'd hate to pull my goddamn gun out and shoot you, Dom, but I will. Just like I would have gladly spent the rest of my life in prison if she had let me shoot that prick she'd been married to. Probably would have done it if she hadn't waited to tell me what shit she'd been through until after she had enough and left his ass. As for taking his money, I had to force the girl to take what was rightfully hers, and in my eyes, it wasn't enough. I was willing to explain earlier, but you know what? I'm not going to explain shit to you. Take the fucking papers and go through them. You're being a dick, and since I'm not in your precious club, I don't have to listen to you rant about something you know nothing about. You need to get out of my office before we both say stuff that can't be taken back."

"Listen to me," I started, but didn't finish when the man's face went bright red.

"Get the fuck out, Dom. I'm done. You don't have a fucking clue, and I'm not feeling much obliged in setting you straight."

"Fine, make a damn fool out of yourself, and while you're at it, find someone else to help you." I stood, threw the envelope back on his desk, and walked out of his office.

"Fucking attorneys. Nothing but a bunch of assholes!" I heard as I pushed through the station's front doors.

My brothers said nothing until I straddled my bike. "Jag, what the hell happened in there? You barrel out and cross the parking lot like you want to kill someone," Coast asked.

"Damn, you and the sheriff didn't get into a fight over the chick, did you?" Flirt asked.

"Sonofabitch, he can have her. The man got bent out of shape when I tried to warn him about getting serious about someone who was more than likely using him for some type of gain. He threw me out of his office after that. Hell, he can learn on his own. I'm done talking. I want a damn beer. No, I want several. I'm getting shitfaced, and I dare anyone to say one goddamned word." I cranked my bike before they asked anything else, and I was on the street and headed toward Soft Tails before they caught up to me.

By the time we reached the parking lot of the club, I'd decided to drink until River's face no longer showed up when I closed my eyes.

It was a helluva plan, and I was damned set on it until I opened the door and walked in.

Fuck me.

Chapter Four

River

In the parking lot at Soft Tails, I sat in my car and stared at the entrance, debating if I should just skip the lunch invitation. After five minutes and a lot of back and forth, I pushed the car door open and slid out of the driver's seat. A deep breath and the beep signaling my car was locked, I started toward the door. Decision made.

Why shouldn't I meet nice people and have a meal? No man could have that type of power over me. Screw him if he had a problem with me being around his friends. Wasn't my issue.

I stepped inside and was surrounded by the sound of voices and music playing low in the background. The place was busy. With my sunglasses pushed up on my head, I gave my eyes time to adjust to the change in lighting before searching for a familiar face. When I made one sweep of the place and thought that Sami and others hadn't gotten there, I saw her stand and wave her arms to get my attention.

Walking toward Sami, I noticed there were only two couples at the table, and as I got closer, Devil rose and pulled over the empty table beside them.

"So glad you made it, River. Grab a seat, and I'll make the introductions," Sami said and smiled.

I refused to the let the sudden butterflies in my stomach influence me. I moved to an empty chair beside Sami. As I reached for the back of the chair, a large hand beat me to it and pulled it out. When I looked up, it was into the smiling face of the older man who lived with Sue, who I had only spoken to in passing. I knew Sue had mentioned his name, but I couldn't remember it. Although I knew he was part of the MC because he wore a leather vest that identified them.

"Have a seat, darlin'." I sat, and he pushed my chair in.

"Thank you," I said as I looked over my shoulder.

"Ah, my pleasure. Any gentleman would have done the same," he replied, then Devil and Kane groaned.

"Goddamn, Roscoe, I would have done it, but you were already there before I got to it," Devil said, then took a seat beside a woman, which I assumed was Bailey since she was the only other woman there besides Sami. "Where did you come from, anyway? It's like you have a built-in radar that goes off when new women are around."

"Well, since Syn has been filling in at the shop while the construction on the club is going on, I get a break. Was going to take lunch home for Sue, but when I called her, she told me you guys already sent the prospect with food since she had Ally and Neely. Which, by the way, my plans for an afternoon slap and tickle session went out the window. So, I figured I'd come here and grab myself lunch. Finding this pretty lady in need of a gentleman's service was just luck," Roscoe said, then glanced at me and winked. When Speed and Devil both pinched the bridge of their noses and shook their heads, and Sami and Bailey laughed, I figured it was typical Roscoe behavior. I couldn't stop my grin because, good grief, the man had to be old enough to be my grandfather.

Speed spoke for the first time since I arrived at the table. "Thanks for that visual, Roscoe. Not sure I'm hungry now, but you're welcome to join us." He used a chin lift to point toward the empty chairs.

"Can we not start? At least give River the brief illusion that we are normal," Sami said, cutting off Roscoe as he opened his mouth to respond.

"I was only going to say, who wouldn't enjoy spending lunch with lovely ladies," Roscoe said as he sat in the chair beside me.

"Normal is overrated," Carly said as she walked up with another man from the club who I hadn't met, but the vest he wore had a nametag on it that read President. When I glanced at the group of people following, I recognized Luna and Ghost, with several other men behind them. As they separated to take seats at the table, the smile left my face. Great. Awesome. Seemed jerk face was joining the group after all.

"Hey, River. Good to see you outside of Yoga Sensual," Luna said as she and Ghost sat across from me.

"Yes, I ran into Sami earlier, and she invited me," I answered as everyone else sat. I refused to look to see where Jag sat. I wasn't going to let him ruin my time.

"I did. And since Roscoe got me sidetracked, let me introduce River to the ones she hasn't met," Sami said, then pointed to Devil. "You met Devil earlier. Beside him is his better half, Bailey." Sami pointed to each person as she worked herself around the table. "You already know Carly. The man beside her is her better half, Crusher, the club's president."

"Seriously, you're supposed to be my BFF and sister at heart," Carly spouted.

"I call it like I see it." Carly stuck her middle finger up at Sami, and Sami chuckled.

I kept the smile on my face even though I felt eyes on me. There wasn't a need to check if I was right. I imagined wherever Jag sat; he was glaring at me.

"Now let me finish. You know Luna and Ghost, River. Beside Ghost is Boss, Turk, Jag, Coast, Flirt, and you already experienced Roscoe."

Every time Sami said one of the men's names, I received a smile and a chin lift in response. Well, except for Jag. He just narrowed his eyes and glared.

"I've passed you coming into my mom's bakery a couple times and wanted to introduce myself, but I was always running late," Bailey said, and I was thankful because it allowed me to look away from Jag.

When I opened my mouth to speak, the waitress interrupted, and the conversation stopped while everyone placed their orders. As soon as she walked away, I looked back at Bailey.

"So, the bakery is your mom's business? I can't go by there without stopping and picking up a couple of cupcakes. Those things are addicting, then after I shove them in my mouth, I feel guilty, so I take an extra yoga class." I chuckled, and Bailey grinned.

"Ally loves them, too. Her favorite is the triple fudge with chocolate icing," Sami said.

"Yes, the chocolate buttercream is delicious. My weakness is the strawberry shortcake with cream cheese icing and sprinkles on top. When I eat them, I swear I can feel my hips expanding."

"Hell, I've seen you leaving the yoga place in those exercise pants. Not a damn thing wrong with your hips, sweetheart."

I felt my cheeks heat, and I glanced to see who had spoken. It was the man sitting beside Roscoe who Sami introduced as Flirt. And I could guess how he came to receive that nickname. Before I replied, the man's head turned, and his focus went to Jag, who sat across from him.

"Asshole, did you seriously just kick me under the table?" Flirt asked, and when I looked at Jag, he was glaring at Flirt.

"Knew lunch was going to be entertaining," Devil commented, and there were a few chuckles from the men around the table. But when I turned my head in his direction, it was in time to see him flinch as Bailey elbowed him. It wasn't the first time I felt as though these people knew something I didn't.

"Sometimes I swear it's like being out with a bunch of overgrown children," Carly said, then shook her head as several of the men grumbled about being included when they hadn't done a thing wrong.

"River, please don't hold the men's behavior against us. They can't seem to help themselves," Luna added.

Ghost moved the arm he had draped on the back of Luna's chair and pulled her to his side. "My behavior this morning wouldn't be considered child-like."

Luna laughed as she smacked his chest and pulled away, sitting straight in her chair again. And when Ghost leaned down and kissed her, I looked away from the open show of affection only to lock eyes with Jag again. The olive skin and dark brown hair were in contrast to the blue of his eyes, but it worked for him. Heck, it worked for me; the man was sinfully gorgeous. We'd gotten off on the wrong foot the first time I'd ran into him and every time after it seemed to worsen. Case in point, our earlier altercation at the sheriff's station.

The men being accused of acting childish had nothing on me with how I've acted around this man. No matter that he was arrogant and got under my skin, I'd been rude. It was time to be the adult and not let what he thought bother me. If he wanted to spend his time glaring at me, then it was his problem, not mine. I broke eye contact and focused my attention back on the other conversations around the table.

Chapter Five

Jag

River smiled and laughed as she talked with Sami and Roscoe. She responded when spoken to, all her actions to someone not paying close attention would look as if she was comfortable with her surroundings. It made me curious if it was just being around my friends or if she was always like this.

I knew a lot of it had to do with me sitting across and down from her. I'd catch her looking at me out of the corner of her eyes, then swiftly go back to acting as if I didn't exist when she saw me watching her.

Good, if I wasn't enjoying myself, why should she? Oh, I kept up with the surrounding conversations. Congratulated Speed and Sami on finding out they were having a son. Told Carly how happy I was she was healed and cleared to go back to work. I even laughed as Ghost and Luna debated the pros and cons of having twin girls versus twin boys. She wasn't far enough along to know yet, but the doctor told them the percentage was high that the twins would be the same sex whether she carried girls or boys. All was done with my jaws clenched and only fleeting glances away from River. The fact she was trying to ignore me wasn't helping. As far as I was concerned, I hadn't done anything wrong. She was the one taking advantage of an older man.

Coast leaned toward me and spoke so only I could hear, "You don't relax, your teeth are going to crack, man."

I cut my eyes to him, then snapped them back to River when she laughed at whatever Sami said. I wasn't sure if I wanted to reach across the table and strangle her or place my hands in her hair to feel the thickness and to see if it was as soft as it looked.

Tipping my bottle of beer and taking a swig, I ignored my brother. I knew I needed to look over the contract for Boss and Turk, but I couldn't get myself together with her sitting across from me.

Once the food came, I figured I would eat and make an excuse to get away from the woman. Go back to my place and work until I pushed her out of my mind. I had to for my sanity.

"Geez, Jag, what the hell? I'm not sure she deserves the death glare you're giving her. She seems nice. Why don't you cut her and yourself a break?"

"You don't know her, Coast," I mumbled, never looking toward him.

"And you do? How many times have you spoken to her besides the few run-ins you've had with her? Because if they went down as you said, then it wasn't an actual conversation."

"Butt the fuck out, Coast," I said, finally turning my head to look at the man.

Coast leaned back in his chair and his eyes scrutinized me, then he snorted, "Holy shit, you're going down, brother. And what's humorous is you don't even know it."

I narrowed my eyes and glared at Coast. "You don't know what you're talking about. Why don't you worry about your own woman problems?"

"Okay, you admitting to having woman problems?" Coast laughed loudly, and several sets of eyes looked in our direction as the table suddenly went quiet.

"What's so funny?" Crusher asked from the other end of the table.

"Our VP being delusional," Flirt said, then looked at me and grinned while Boss and Turk both coughed to cover up their chuckles. Assholes. And evidently, Coast and I hadn't spoken as low as we thought. When I glanced at River, I knew the blank look on her face verified she'd heard us, too.

"Nah, I got the full picture today. I'm far from delusional," I said, never taking my eyes away from River. I refused to feel guilty.

River shook her head, looked down, and I watched her take a deep breath before she pushed back her chair and stood. She reached into the pocket of her jeans and pulled out folded bills.

"Thanks for inviting me, Sami, but I think it's best if I leave. This should cover the food I ordered." River laid a couple of bills down and shoved the rest back in her pocket. "It was nice meeting everyone," she added as she stepped away from the table.

Sami glared at me and then stood. "River, please don't go. It's been really nice getting to know you." I received the evil eye from the rest of the women as they chimed in to agree with Sami. Then Sami's voice lowered, and I caught the end of her sentence, "...being an asshole."

River nodded and walked away without another word. I ran a hand down my face before I looked around the table. My brothers were staring at me with various expressions on their faces, and I would undoubtedly hear more than I wanted to once River was out of earshot.

Speed helped Sami sit back down, and before anyone could speak, the food arrived. Candie must have sensed the tension at the table because she didn't say a word. She moved around the table until everyone had what they ordered, then she mentioned bringing back refills and walked away.

Before they could pounce, I spoke, "I know I was rude to her, but none of you know—"

"Rude! I think the word you are looking for is dick," Luna said.

"Luna," Ghost said and didn't get another word out.

"Oh, don't Luna me. He was acting like a dick. He spent the entire time glaring at her. I can't be the only one who noticed. She even tried to ignore him and enjoy herself, but no, he continued with whatever the fuck he thought he was doing. That woman has been nothing but nice and polite when I've talked with her at Yoga Sensual. She's on the reserved side until you get her talking. She didn't deserve to be treated that way."

"No shit. She should have reached across the table and slapped the snot out of you. That's what I would've done," Carly commented.

"Carly," Crusher's voice carried a warning.

"I know he is the VP, but that doesn't give him a pass on being an asshole," Carly said, disgustedly.

Crusher looked at me. "Brother, that was bad and totally unlike you."

"Why would you treat her like that, Dom?" Sami asked, and the hurt on her face was palpable. Looking at Speed, his expression read 'fix it'. My brother did not like his woman upset.

"I've never seen you treat a woman so poorly," Bailey added.

"You might be mad at me now, but you will thank me later. She probably would've ended up trying to use you women as she's using the sheriff." I wouldn't apologize for looking out for everyone.

"Using the sheriff?" Roscoe asked with a frown.

"Yes, she is. We," I waved to include the others, "stopped by the station before we came here and saw her and him embracing on the sidewalk. She moved here to be close to him," I said what I could without going into the sheriff's business of wanting to make sure he provided for her.

"Okay, I'm not sure how you see that as using the sheriff. I mean daughters hug their fathers, and some have been known to move closer to a parent," Roscoe said and sat his hamburger down as if he hadn't dropped a bomb, and not only on me, by the looks on everyone else's faces.

"Daughter," I whispered.

"Yeah, a daughter. When Will and Jillian divorced, Jillian moved back east and took River with her. I guess she was about five then. The girl looks just like her mo—"

"Sonofabitch!" I cut Roscoe off and stood so fast I knocked my chair over. I didn't even bend to pick it up as I headed for the door. The others' voices could be heard, but I couldn't focus on what they said. I had to get to River.

When I hit the parking lot, I searched for her car, spotting it just as it started. I took off at a run, and as the car moved backward, I had the passenger door open. River startled and slammed the brakes on. The abrupt stop had me grabbing hold of the frame along with the door to keep me from being knocked to the pavement.

"Have you lost your damn mind!?"

I plopped down into the seat, which was a chore because the car wasn't made for a man my size, and immediately reached to rub my knees after smacking them on the glove box.

"Damn, they don't give you much room in here," I said as I reached for the lever to adjust the seat. Even sliding it all the way back, I couldn't stretch out my legs.

"No one asked you to get in, so why don't you get out?"

"No."

"No?"

"At least not until we talk. And then you can come back in and eat your lunch."

River stared at me, and I noticed for the first time a faint splatter of freckles across her nose, along with how the green of her eyes darkened when she was irritated. And she was irritated with me. Which she had every right to be.

"Are you on medication?" The tone she asked in was flat, and it had my lips twitching. "There is nothing funny about this. You are arrogant, mean, and I refuse to let you continue to humiliate me! And if you think I would go back inside with you to eat after what you did to me in there already, I suggest you tell your doctor you need an adjustment to your meds because they aren't working correctly."

"There's that snotty tone. It gets to me every time and leaves me irritated because I'm not sure which bothers me most—that you get under my skin or that it makes me hard and all I want to do is strip you down, spread you wide, and see if you taste as tart as your voice. Or is between your thighs and your mouth in contrast with each other: one bold and sharp while the other is sweet with just enough salty flavor to keep me wanting to come back for more," I said in a low voice and watched River's eyes deepen into the darkest green while her breathing picked up enough I could physically see her pulse beating on the side of her neck.

"What do you want from me, Dom?" River asked, her voice barely above a whisper. At least I knew I affected her as much as she affected me.

"I'm not sure, but let's start with this." Lost in her eyes, I moved and did what I had wanted from the first time I saw her.

I cupped her head with my hands, and my fingers weaved through her hair until the thing that held the mass unclipped and released the strands and cascaded down her shoulders. I was right. It was thick and soft to the touch. I pulled her forward as I leaned in and paused to give her the chance to pull away. When she didn't move, I closed the remaining distance and touched my lips to hers.

The kiss was gentle until I ran my tongue over her lips and received the first small taste of her. Nipping her bottom lip, she opened, then I plunged. Nothing I dreamed, nothing I had ever experienced, came close to actually having River. Every crevice brought more of her flavor, and when she moaned as her tongue explored, then melted into me as close as the console between us would allow, I knew nothing would keep me away from her. Whether or not she was meant to be mine, I wanted to explore whatever seemed to be between us to see if she was everything I ever wanted.

The only obstacle I might face would be to get her to admit she felt the same way. Especially after how we'd started out.

Breaking the kiss, I leaned my forehead against hers and worked on leveling my breath. When was the last time a woman had turned me inside out?

"So, the sheriff is your dad, huh?" River released the edges of my cut that she'd latched on to while we were kissing and pushed at my chest. I gave her the space she seemed to need and sat back in the car's seat.

"Figured that out, did you?"

"Roscoe brought it to my attention. How long were you going to let me think you two were romantically involved?"

"Don't blame me because you made assumptions." I grinned, and she glared. "And stop grinning!"

"You're going to keep me on my toes, aren't you?" My grin grew when her eyes narrowed.

"I won't keep you on anything. This..." River waved between us, "shouldn't have happened, and I plan for it not to happen again."

"Bullshit. If you ask me, everything between us led up to that kiss, and you enjoyed it just as much as I did."

River huffed. "Who doesn't enjoy a pleasant kiss?"

"Now you're trying to piss me off. Pleasant, my ass. Five more seconds and I could've had you across this console and riding me if I hadn't broken the kiss."

"Please, in your dreams."

"Oh, you have been, but I think I'm going to enjoy reality a whole lot more. And so will you." I unfolded myself out of the car and leaned down so I could see River's face. "You need to go home and think about what you want. You've pushed buttons I didn't know I had. Now I'm over it. We are going to explore what the hell this is between us."

"I don't have to think. There is nothing between us. Besides, I don't want any of this. A relationship wasn't in my plans!"

"Yeah, well, tough shit. Plans change. Drive safe." I slammed the car door shut before she could say anything else. Before I could walk around the car, the window rolled down.

"You really are an asshole, Dom."

I paused. She really was working toward pissing me off. But instead of letting it show, I turned my head in her direction and grinned. "Yeah, but, sweetheart, I'm going to be your asshole," I said, and bent enough to wink at her before I walked around the car toward the bar.

"Seriously, get your meds adjusted!" River yelled out of the driver's side window.

"Sure thing," I said over my shoulder, then stopped and looked back at her. "And, sweetheart, would you let me get inside before you pull out—I'd like to see where this is going between us and I'm not sure how many more times I can avoid your attempts to run over me." I continued to the door as Coast stepped out in time to hear River yell jerk out the window before she peeled out of the lot.

With the look on Coast's face, I threw my head back and laughed.

"You okay? I came to check if everything was alright out here."

"Couldn't be better, brother. Let's go inside. I'm suddenly hungry." I slapped Coast on the back and pulled the door open, feeling more like myself than I had in a long time.

Chapter Six

River

"Ugh, that man! *Go home and think about it.* Whatever. Like one hot as hell kiss was a reason to dive into a relationship," I said as I finally could move my car up to the fast-food restaurant's speaker and place my order. I'd only been in line for twenty minutes, which was another thing to blame on the jerk.

Leaving the drive-thru lane, I reached in the bag and snatched a fry, shoving it in my mouth before I pulled out onto main street. As I drove down the road, I shoveled more fries in my mouth to curb my growling stomach, but the food did nothing for my temper. I wasn't sure there was anything that could.

I scrunched the top of the bag together and pushed down a little more on the gas pedal. I planned to stop at the bakery, pick up dessert for dinner with my dad, then go home and eat. Putting Dom and his kiss behind me.

Reaching the block where the bakery was located, I missed the open spot to park in the front. So I circled the block with the hope it would remain available. When I saw it was still empty, I pulled my car up beside the car in front of the free spot and placed my car in reverse. I hated parallel parking, but I could admit that a compact car was an advantage. It made it easier to pull into the small spaces.

I turned the wheel and hit the gas to back into the spot. No sooner than I had the car halfway into the spot, I heard the thump as something hit my car and I slammed on the brakes.

I looked over my shoulder when I heard several voices yell, "What the fucking hell," as a few men dove for the sidewalk. I finished parking my car, took a deep breath, and opened my door and eased out.

"Are you okay?" I asked as I walked around the car to the sidewalk and looked the men over to see if I had hit either of them. That's when I noticed the vest they wore. I didn't have to see the patch on the back to know that were Black Hawk MC members. That was the kind of luck I had. Could this day get any worse?

"Holy hell, thank God my reflexes are good, or I'd be answering your question with a big ole negative." The one who spoke had dark brown hair and matching eyes that were currently narrowed at me.

"If I didn't hit you, then what was the thud I heard?" I glanced at my car and didn't notice any damage or anything lying on the ground that I could have hit.

"Probably my hand when I smacked the side of the car before I jumped back. Damn, where'd you learn to drive?" was asked by the man who spoke before.

"Sorry, I was watching to make sure I didn't hit the other car as I was backing in, and I didn't see you."

"That's why cars have mirrors," said another of the men.

"Cut her some slack, Cruz. If it was our time to be taken out, at least it would have been by a beautiful woman."

"If it had been your ass she damn near took out, you wouldn't be flirting with the girl, Romeo."

"Like that is even possible for him, Flyboy. Even if she's young enough to be his daughter."

"Yeah, Stroker, as if that makes a difference."

The men chuckled while I stood there and stared.

"Quit harassing River, you old fools." I turned my head to the feminine voice, and Claire stood in the doorway of her shop. I hadn't even noticed she had opened the door with my attention focused on the older men and their banter. It surprised me a little that she remembered my name, not as if I was in her shop every single day.

"Now, darlin', we're not bothering the pretty woman. She almost ran over Flyboy," one man said and walked toward Claire.

Finally, as I stood there while the man and Claire spoke, my brain kicked back in gear.

"Why would you just step off the sidewalk? You should've made sure no car was moving into the spot," I pointed at my car, "before you stepped into the street. Bad enough you're crossing in the middle of the block, which I presume was to get to the bikes parked across the street," I said and looked between the men.

"Excuse me, sweetheart, but why didn't *you* use your mirrors? They're there for a purpose other than to see to put on make-up," the one they called Flyboy, who I almost hit, snapped back.

"Why didn't *you* go to the corner to cross? You know, since that is where the *crosswalk* is... sweetheart," I said snottily because I had had my fill of bikers for the day. Before Flyboy could respond, one of the other men who hadn't spoken stepped between us.

I took a few steps back and looked up at the man now in front. The smile on his face caught me off guard.

"Do you find this funny?" I lifted a brow and asked the man, which only caused his smile to widen.

"No, ma'am. You're Will's daughter, aren't you?" he asked while I stared at him.

"Excuse me?" I asked, confused about the sudden change in the conversation. If you could call what was taking place a conversation to begin with.

"Oh my gosh, I can't believe I missed it before. You look just like Jillian," Claire said, and I looked at her.

"You know my mother?"

"Yes, we went to school together. I remember when she married your dad. Even as a child, you were as beautiful as you are now." Claire smiled.

"Thank you," I replied. I wanted to know more about my time here as a child but couldn't bring myself to ask. I was five when my mother and dad divorced and didn't remember much about the time I lived in Shades Valley or my parents together in general.

"Knew Will's daughter had moved back. Even seen you around town, just never put the two together until now," the man who stood in front of me said, then stepped to the side.

The other men nodded in agreement with the man who they called Preacher. After they introduced themselves, they even told me how they knew my mother and dad. As the conversation went on, the near accident confrontation was forgotten. At least I'd thought.

"Well, seems you have it out for the Amara men, River," Romeo said. He stood by Claire and, from the way he touched her, gave the impression they were familiar with each other.

"Huh?" I frowned at Romeo, and he chuckled. "What are you talking about?" I asked, then felt the blush when what he said registered, and my eyes flew to Flyboy. When he introduced himself before, I hadn't really paid that close of attention to their last names. He'd said to call him Flyboy, but his name was Tony Amara. And I thought the day couldn't have gotten any worse. Yeah, it seemed it could.

"Hmm... explains a lot of my son's moods lately," Flyboy said and grinned. "And getting a good look at you, I can see why."

"Really? After meeting you, I can see where he gets his... personality," I said, then looked at the other men when they chuckled.

"Oh yeah, I definitely understand. Going to enjoy watching this play out." Flyboy chuckled as the others agreed with him.

"Leave the poor girl alone," Claire said, then looked at me. "Were you coming to the bakery, River?" I looked at Claire, thankful for her cutting in and changing the subject.

"Yes, I am. I can't seem to stay away from your shop. I'm going to have to join a few more of Willa's classes," I said and walked toward the entrance to the bakery.

"Sweetheart, the way you and Willa look, that yoga crap works."

I glanced over my shoulder to see which man had spoken, then at Preacher once I noticed the other men looking at him with various expressions on their faces.

"Well, well, that is interesting," Claire mumbled so low I was the only one who heard.

"If we are going to get in a few hours of riding, let's go. And when we stop, Preacher can explain the last part of his statement," Stroker said, then turned to Claire and me. "Nice meeting you, River. Claire, see you later."

"That's my cue, darlin'," Romeo said, then bent and kissed Claire on the forehead before he followed the others as they moved off the sidewalk and stood behind my car.

"Hey, you were almost run over, don't you think you should use the crosswalk?" Claire yelled as the men stepped out on main street.

My mouth dropped open when Flyboy yelled over his shoulder, "Nah, we're good. River's with you and not behind the wheel!"

Claire chuckled. "Come on, honey, let's get you taken care of." I turned and followed Claire into her bakery.

Twenty minutes later, I was walking into my house with my now cold burger and fries and the freshly baked apple pie that was my dad's favorite. I placed everything on the counter, then heated the hamburger in the microwave while I tossed the remaining fries in the trash. As I sat on the stool to eat, I looked at the clock on the wall. I had enough time when I finished to pick up the house and the mess I left in my bedroom before I needed to start on dinner. Or more importantly, enough stuff to do to keep my mind from wandering to Dom and the kiss that made me want more.

I just finished hanging the clothes I'd thrown on my bed when the doorbell rang. I walked down the stairs and looked through the peephole on the front door to see Sami standing on the other side.

"Hi, River. Hope I'm not bothering you," Sami said, and smiled when I opened the door.

I smiled back. "No, not at all. Would you like to come in?" I asked and stepped back.

"I can't. I need to pick Ally and Neely up at Sue's, but I wanted to come over and apologize for lunch."

"Not a problem, Sami. You couldn't have known Dom would be a jerk. I should've just ignored him and been the adult, instead of acting as childish as he was acting." Sami's snort was unexpected.

"Please, you acted better than most women would have. And I'm not saying this to make you upset, but I know you and Jag have had a few run-ins." Sami put her hand up, stopping my reply. "Not the details. I just know that he hasn't been himself since the day he met you in town for me. River, the encounters you've had with him, I don't know anything to say other than his behavior is so out of character for him. Dom is one of the most laid-back men I know. Well, until he's around you."

"Sami, where are you going with this? Are you asking me to stay away from him? Warning me off? I'm not following, which doesn't matter, really. The man is..."

"Irritating? A pain in the ass? Arrogant? Bossy? A smartass? A jerk?"

I couldn't help it. I laughed, and Sami did, too.

"Ah, so you know him well?" I asked jokingly.

"I'm sorry, River. I'm handling this all wrong. What I should have said was we—me, Bailey, Luna, and Carly really like you and hope you won't hold today against us. I came over to ask if you'd like to join us the day after tomorrow on a shopping excursion?"

I thought of the women I had met, and regardless of whatever was going on, or not going on between Dom and me, I liked them. They were nice and seemed fun to be around.

"A girls' only shopping trip?"

"Yes," Sami said, and smiled. "And please don't hold what I said before against me?"

"Hey, Dom is all those things."

"True, but I wasn't referring to that. Lately, Dom has just been... I'm not sure if troubled is the right word or not."

"Assholish?" I suggested.

"That will work." Sami chuckled. "I wasn't trying to warn you off or take up for him. I just wanted you to know that isn't his normal behavior."

"Okay, so should I meet you and the others somewhere for the outing?"

"Oh, I'm glad you're coming. It'll be fun. Why don't we meet you here, say ten?"

"I'll be ready."

"Fantastic. Well, I better get back to Sue's and get the girls. See ya, River."

"Bye, Sami," I said and watched as she walked to Sue's house before I closed the door. Once in the kitchen, I pulled out the things I needed and started on dinner.

"I'm stuffed. That was great, honey. Thank you," my dad said, and I grinned as he pushed his plate away.

"Well, that is terrible. Who's going to eat the pie?" I asked as I got up from the table, picking our empty plates up. Once I placed them in the sink, I grabbed the pie off the counter and set it on the table.

"If you keep feeding me like this, I'm going to need bigger uniforms."

I smiled when he pushed his chair back and went to the cabinet, grabbed a couple of small plates and a knife before he joined me back at the table. After I cut us each a slice, I set my dad's piece in front of him, and he groaned when he took his first bite.

"I'll remember that next time I cook and leave out the dessert part of the meal," I said as I scooped up my first bite.

"Hey! Not on my account. I could use new uniforms."

I shook my head as I brought the next fork full to my mouth. We finished the pie in silence, then my dad insisted on helping me clean the kitchen.

"Want to sit on the patio for a bit, or do you need to head home?" I asked as I handed him the last pan to dry.

"I'd love to. Need to let that delicious meal settle."

After pouring us each another glass of tea, we headed out the back door to the patio.

"This is nice," I said, and used the toe of my shoe to kick the patio swing in motion.

"It is, for several reasons," my dad said and put his arm around me and squeezed. "Having you here is the best part, River. I know the circumstances that brought you here suck, but I refuse to dwell on them. I'm too damn happy that you're here. I'm tempted to call Thomas and thank him for fucking up."

"Dad," I said and rested my head on his shoulder. We rocked back and forth quietly, not sure how long we stayed in our own thoughts.

"So..." Dad began, then cleared his throat, "How did the rest of your day go?" His tone had me lifting my head to look at him. What I saw made me smile.

"Boy, that face and your eyes just gave me a brief look at what growing up here with you as the sheriff would have been like. I wouldn't have gotten by with much, would I have?"

"What, you think because you're grown, it makes a difference?" I watched his jaw tighten while he stared back at me. I couldn't imagine anyone holding up under his scrutiny.

"You can't be serious?" He lifted his brow at my question but didn't answer.

No way could he know what happened at lunch or in front of the bakery. For once, I did what I said and hadn't thought of Dom.

"Gee, okay. Dom showed up at lunch, and it didn't go well. But if I'm going to be honest, some blame is on me. The man gets under my skin and then I act like a spoiled teenager. Then I wanted to get your favorite pie, and I almost took out Dom's dad, Flyboy, in front of the bakery. And he and I might have said a few smartass things to each other. There, happy?"

"You wouldn't have gotten away with anything," Dad said and laughed when I stared at him. "Don't feel bad, honey. Many people crack easily."

"You knew nothing, and I told you?"

"I didn't say that. I knew basically what happened at Soft Tails because Dom stopped by the station to pick some paperwork up from me. He told me, and he took all the blame. Said his behavior was rude, and he had no excuse for it. But running over his dad—that I didn't know." Dad chuckled. "God, River, his father? Should I be worried that you have it out for the Amara men?"

"It isn't funny." I plopped back on the swing and crossed my arms over my chest. "The other men accused me of that, too."

"Other men?"

"Yeah. Romeo, Preacher, Stroker, Cruz."

"Thanks for the heads up. I'm sure I'll catch shit when I see them again."

"Why would they say anything to you? I'm the one who backed into the spot, but in my defense, they shouldn't have been crossing the street from there!" I turned my head and looked at my dad when he started laughing.

"Did you tell them that?" I nodded, and he laughed harder. At my glare, he got himself under control and continued. "I'm sorry, honey. I wasn't laughing at you. I was laughing, thinking of Stroker's and the others' faces. They aren't used to having people stand up to them. But I guess with the women their sons are pairing off with, maybe they're learning to take things in stride."

"You said Dom came by to pick up papers, wasn't that what he came by for earlier?"

"Well... we had a minor disagreement before." I furrowed my brows at him but didn't speak. "Fine, he pissed me off, and we had words. Then he left. He came back to apologize."

"Dad, I'm sorry I put you in the middle. It wasn't fair to you. He throws me off balance, and I don't like that feeling."

"Come here," Dad said, and pulled me back to his side. "I've tried over the years to let you live without interference from me. Mainly because I didn't feel like I had the right to since I was only around for a short time each summer. From a distance, I watched you grow into a beautiful, smart woman. I also noticed the struggle with you trying to find your way, instead of what your mother expected of you. Then you married Thomas right out of college, and I felt I missed the opportunity to exert any advice. My life was here. I never wanted to move. Your mother wanted to be anywhere but here. And the one person who we both should have protected paid the price for her and my decisions. I should've fought to keep you closer than giving in and letting your mother take you across the country."

"Dad." He squeezed my shoulder.

"Let me finish. Yes, I spent vacation time with you, but I should have insisted you spend your summers here. Instead, I listened to your mother about how it would disrupt the structure of your childhood. That idiotic shit is on me. I love you, River, and I hope you know I would do anything to see you happy."

"I love you, too, Dad. And I'm getting there. Don't worry about me. I'm settled in the house and looking forward to starting my teaching job. I'm even going shopping with Sami, Bailey, Carly, and Luna. This feels like home to me, even though I didn't grow up here. And a lot of that has to do with you being here. You might feel you've let me down, but I never have." I tilted my head and kissed his cheek.

Sometime during us talking, the swing stopped, so I gave it a push to start it back up.

"Going to tell me what's going on between you and Dom?"

"What happened to not interfering?"

"I think I said *tried*. That was before. You're here now. So..."

"Honestly, Dad, I'm not sure. After Thomas, I don't know if I can trust my feelings. And Dom is confusing. One minute, he acts as though he is irritated I breathe the same air, then he is kissing me, and I—" I stopped talking when I realized what I let slip.

"What the hell, River?"

I sat up straight to see my dad's face. He was pinching the bridge of his nose between his fingers and had his eyes closed. I watched as he lowered his hand, then took a deep breath before he opened his eyes.

"Dad?"

"Give me a minute."

The way he spoke had me grinning. This was the side of my dad I missed out on when I grew up and started dating. "Take all the minutes you need. But, Dad, you know I've been kissed and—"

"Stop! I know somewhere in my mind that you're a grown woman who has been married. I get what that entails, *but...* knowing and hearing about it as the woman's father doesn't work well. Yes, when I look at you, I see an adult," he moved his hand to his heart, "in here, you will always be my little girl. It is also the place where there will never be a man good enough for you. With that said, I know you're unsure of yourself because of that cheating ass son-of-a-bitch pansy you were married to."

"Don't hold back how you feel, Dad," I said, and when he glared at me, I couldn't stop from smiling.

"Smartass. Everything I said about him is true. But back to you. Don't let what happened with him keep you from finding happiness with another man. Whether it's Dom, or someone else. Know that I will be happy when you do. I just don't want to share in the details."

"I'll try. Not sure I'm ready, though."

"You'll know when you are. Don't let anyone push you if you aren't."

"I can't say it enough. Coming here was the best decision I've made in a long time."

"I'm glad you made it, too. Now, how about feeding me another piece of that apple pie before your old dad heads home?"

"You got it. Come on, I might be swayed to make you some coffee to go with it."

My dad stood and held out his hand. I grabbed ahold, and he pulled me up, then we headed into the house.

"You're the best daughter," my dad said when I started the coffee.

"I'm your only daughter."

He laughed as I had wanted. Spending time with my dad these last couple of months had been the best. Now, if I only knew what to do about Dom, but that could wait. I had plenty of time.

Chapter Seven

Jag

Up, showered, dressed, and ready for the day to start, I sat at the table with my coffee as the sun was rising. Flipping through the last of the sheriff's documents, I made notations to the side with my suggestions for him to go over.

I'd gone back to his office yesterday and apologized for what had taken place between us earlier. Will Lance was a good man, a good sheriff, and always fair, but tough. So after we talked it out, and he said, "I know a lot of places to hide a body," he meant it.

The knock on my back door had me turning to see Coast through the window, and I rose, turned the lock, then grabbed an extra mug as he walked in.

"Saw your light on. Glad to know I'm not the only one not sleeping," Coast said as a greeting and reached for the coffee mug I held out to him.

"Yeah, well, at least I got some work done," I said, pointing to the stack of papers as we sat down. "What's keeping you up?"

"Same old shit creeping up. Weeks go by and nothing, then something triggers it and bam... a few nights reliving missions I wish could have ended differently. Guess I should be thankful it only hits every so often."

"I can't relate, but I've read about PTSD and dealt with a few soldiers who suffered with it as they dealt in court because of their actions," I said as I gathered the sheets of paper and slid them back into the envelope.

"Vicious cycle. Wouldn't wish any of it on my worst enemy," Coast said and got up and grabbed the coffeepot and brought it to the table. "We didn't have time to talk yesterday about what happened with you and River, between helping set up the equipment at the gym and making sure the massage side is ready to go. Is that the reason you're up at the butt crack of dawn?"

I reached for the coffeepot, filled my cup, then leaned back in my chair and took a drink. My brother sat quietly and waited me out.

"Have you ever felt that if you don't do something right, you won't get a second chance?"

"I guess. When my team was sent out on missions, the pressure was there that one screw up would cost us. You can't make someone undead, regardless of what they sometimes portray in movies. What is going on with you, Jag? You were acting like your old self when we went back inside to finish lunch yesterday."

"She gets to me, Coast. And I'm not sure why because we butt heads every time we are around each other. Yet there's something about her... Christ, I feel like a teenager who wants the girl but doesn't want to get crushed if she doesn't want him," I said, bent my head and rubbed the back of my neck. Coast chuckling had my heading snapping up.

"You know, I've got endless hours of enjoyment watching Speed, Crusher, Devil, and even Ghost stumble around their women. You, Flirt, and I have discussed and laughed about it at their expense. We also said we wouldn't make the same mistakes, so stop thinking about messing it up. If you want to see if there's anything between you two, then go for it. Because if there is something there, a few mistakes along the way will be worth it in the end. God knows I've got my own issues to work through with Mac, but watching how River gets you fired up—must mean something. If I were you, I wouldn't give her too much time to think."

"Like you've done with Mac?"

"Pretty much. So don't be an asshat. If she is yours, go after her until she's convinced." Coast got up and placed his coffee cup in the sink, then looked at me when he opened the door. "Only thing planned today is cleaning up the businesses and checking in on the renovations at Soft Tails. Bet you could think of something else to do." Coast grinned, and I laughed.

"Yeah, I have a few ideas."

Coast grinned. "Well, I'll tell the others you had something else pressing today," he said, then walked out. Before the door closed behind him, I heard, "And another one down."

Laughing, I walked to the sink and washed the few dishes that sat inside. By the time I finished, I knew exactly what I wanted to do. If I dropped by the sheriff's station first and went over my notes with Will, the sun would have had time to warm the air.

I grabbed the envelope off the table, snagged my keys, and headed out the door toward my bike. There was a plan to start.

"You didn't have to rush with those, Dom," Sheriff Lance said when I dropped the envelope on his desk.

"No problem. If you have time now, we could go over my suggestions, then I can get the changes fixed for you." I sat in the chair in front of his desk.

"Sure." He opened the envelope, pulled out the paperwork, and flipped through. "You're out early."

"Yeah, figured I would get these to you and give the day a chance to warm up."

"You guys going riding today?" Will asked while he continued to look over the papers.

"No, just me. I planned to ride today and take River with me. Figured she would enjoy the ride a little better if it were warmer." Will frowned at my statement but didn't look up. "You going to have a problem if I pursue River?"

When he didn't reply, I waited quietly until he finished with the papers and finally looked up at me.

"She's my daughter, Dom. I love her, and I don't want to see her hurt again."

Will stopped me from speaking when he raised his hand.

"I went to River's for dinner, and she and I talked about a few things, including the two of you. When you and I worked through our issue yesterday, I told you her ex was an asshole, but I didn't go into details, and I won't. That is for River to share with you if she chooses. Because of him and his choices, she's going to be more cautious. He was embarrassed, and mentality put her through hell. I know she comes across as a woman who seems to have no problem handling herself, but, Dom, it's a shield she has placed around her for years. River went from her mother, Jillian, and Alfred's home to the one she shared with Thomas when they married after she graduated college. This is the first time she's been on her own, and really living in the real world. Instead of the privileged one her mother kept her sheltered in.

"I don't mean to dump this crap on you, but I think you need to know a little background. River's mother, Jillian, was raised by her father. Her mother died when she was ten from complications dealing with pneumonia. Her father was a heart surgeon at the hospital. Jillian and I met in high school and began dating. When Jillian was preparing to go to college, they offered her dad Chief of Surgery at some hospital in Connecticut. She didn't want to move because of me, so we married. I was a new deputy then and making hardly any money. Oh, we were young and in love, so at first that didn't bother Jillian. She even got a job as a bank teller to help. Within a year, she was pregnant.

"After River was born, Jillian quit her job and stayed home because daycare would have eaten up her check, anyway. We didn't have a lot of money to spare, but she didn't seem to mind. I was at work more than home because I would take extra shifts to pick up more money. The turning point was when her dad died in an automobile accident, and Jillian was his sole heir. River was almost five. I came home one day, and Jillian asked for a divorce. To make a long story short, I didn't see it coming, and it threw me for a loop. I didn't fight her about taking River thousands of miles away from me when she said they were moving into the house her dad had owned and she had inherited. I just went along with it. Not long after, they moved again when Jillian met Alfred and they married. Jillian sold her dad's home, and River was uprooted to Alfred's house.

"I spent my vacation time going to see River because I believed Jillian when she said River's life shouldn't be derailed every summer to come here."

"Will, what's this about? Are you trying to tell me River is like her mom and she might get involved with me, but then bolt because I'm not wealthy," I interrupted because I wasn't sure I understood where he was going by telling me all this. And I wanted to because it would help me understand River better.

"God, no. River may look like her mother, but she is not even close to being like her. Jillian enjoys being the center of attention and having money to do anything she wishes. She enjoys the prestige she receives from being married to an attorney who is a partner in a large law firm. River never rocked the boat with anything her mother suggested. Birthday parties, a sweet sixteen party, a graduation party bigger than most couples' weddings. It was ridiculous, and River really never enjoyed or wanted lavishness. She would have been happy with a homemade cake and her classmates playing stupid birthday party games."

"I get when she was little, she didn't have much say, but when she was a teenager, why didn't she revolt against what her mother wanted to do?" I asked, because frankly what I'd seen of the woman. She gave as good as she got.

"Because by then, she'd put up a shield to deal. It was easier for her than the argument it would have caused between her and her mother."

"So not only is she unsure of herself, but she also wears a shield to hide her true self?"

"Yes, the real her is underneath. I've gotten peeks of her. I'm just not sure she knows how to let her fully out," Will said, and leaned back in his chair.

"Is this your way of warning me not to push her, but to take it slow and easy until she finds her way?" I asked and cocked a brow at him.

"Last month, hell, a few days ago, I might have said that. But watching the two of you yesterday, I've never seen her go at someone like that. Before she would have shut down, accepted what you said, even if it pissed her off. After, she would have avoided you from then on to avoid any confrontation."

"Exactly what are you saying, Will?" It surprised me when Will smiled.

"I've known you your whole life. You're confident of what you want out of life. You play by your rules, but you're fair, loyal, and not easily deterred when you've set your mind on something. Every one of those traits served you well in the military and is making you a great vice president for Black Hawk. So, I'm telling you to push with River. Break through the wall and help her step out into the world as she should have a long time ago. I won't stick my nose in what goes on between the two of you, well, as long as you don't do something stupid. The only thing I ask, Dom, is if you decide to push her, make sure you want a relationship with her. I'm not saying marriage. Hell, she just got out of one. I'm saying don't go after her because you like the challenge she brings and once it's gone, you're gone. Because if she lets you in and you aren't willing to put in the time, I'm not sure she will ever bother to try again. And I want my daughter to be happy. She deserves it."

"Will, I can't guarantee forever. I don't know River. But I'm interested enough to get to know her and see what this pull between her and I is," I said as honestly as I could since he was being more than open with me.

"That's all I can ask," Will said and leaned forward, resting his arms on his desk.

"I'll do my best not to hurt her. And if I do, know it won't be intentional."

"Fair enough. How about we go through your notes since I've taken up part of your morning? I only have a couple of questions. Everything you suggested looks good."

I stood and moved to stand beside Will so I could view the documents with him.

"One last thing, Dom," Will said, looking up at me. "If the two of you decide to get together, I don't want to know any specifics. Some things fathers don't need to know. When a man has a daughter, he sleeps better without that knowledge."

"Sure thing," I said, then chuckled.

"Appreciate it."

I placed my hand on Will's shoulder and squeezed before I leaned closer to read where he pointed.

The sooner we finished, the sooner I could head to River's.

Chapter Eight

River

I heard a motorcycle and walked to the window in the living room and looked out to see Dom pulling into my driveway and a car passing by.

Did the man not have any manners? Who just showed up at someone's house at nine in the morning. Thank God I'd showered and changed out of my pajamas. Not that yoga pants and a tank were any different from the sweats and oversized shirt I slept in.

I watched him dismount, then remove his helmet and set it on the seat. He turned toward the road, and I followed his direction to where a car was moving down the street before turning the corner.

When Dom turned around and started for the front door, I ducked from the window, not wanting to be caught. Instead of ringing the bell, he knocked, and I moved to the door. Before I opened it, I straightened the hem of my shirt, then ran my hands nervously down my thighs. With one deep breath, I pulled the door open.

"Dom, what are you doing here?" I asked as he looked me over.

"You're an intelligent woman, River."

Before I had a chance to reply, he placed his hands on my hips and moved me back as he stepped through the doorway. Once he was inside, he released me, kicked the door shut, then cupped my face between his hands and leaned down until his lips were aligned with mine.

"You've got two seconds to tell me no before I kiss you," he said, and I felt the warmth from his breath at his closeness.

What I saw in his eyes had my stomach tightening, and I licked my lips at their sudden dryness. The kiss we shared in my car had been unexpected, and by the time I'd gotten past the shock of it, it was over. This kiss would be more, and though I still wasn't sure if I wanted anything to do with the man in front of me, I went to my toes and closed the distance.

I made the move, but was not the one to control the kiss. In the meeting of our lips, Dom turned us, and I found myself with my back against the door.

His lips were warm, and when his tongue demanded entrance, I complied by opening to him. Our tongues met and dueled while we explored each other's mouths. Dom tasted of coffee with a hint of mint and the flavors had me wanting to experience more of him. At some point, as the kiss continued, I placed my hands at his waist and held on for support. With his body pressed against mine, I couldn't help but feel his hardness. It was then I realized I had a choice to make, not because of Dom's words from the day before—no, it was because I needed to decide if I could put my past hurt aside and take a chance with this man.

Thomas's deceit and actions had hurt me, but, Dom, though we really didn't know each other well, I knew if I let him in and he hurt me, it ultimately could destroy me.

Was I willing to risk it? Willing to take a chance to see if what I felt with him was more than just lust or something to take away the loneliness that being single and on my own for the first time? Could I live with the regret for the unknown because I let my fear of failure with another man fuel my decision?

Dom broke the kiss and looked into my eyes as we both fought to catch our breaths. The blue in his eyes had darkened with desire. Desire for me. I didn't want to compare him to Thomas after what we shared, but it didn't escape me that not once had Thomas ever looked at me with such need.

"You need to go put on jeans and a sweatshirt or grab a jacket. Or my decision to get to know you before this," Dom dropped his hands from my face and waved between us, "goes further, will be tossed and I will carry you upstairs to your bedroom and get to know you on a whole different level. And if the kiss was any indication, our sexual experience will be explosive."

"Why do I need to change?" I asked and shook my head to clear it.

"Because I want to spend the day with you, and we are going to be on my bike."

"Excuse me."

"Go change, River. I thought we could spend the day together. I want to take you out on my bike. But if you want to stay here, in the house, where we can get to know each in private...instead of in public—"

I wasn't sure if Dom had anything else to say. I cut him off before he had the chance. "Fine. But you could have asked instead of being bossy," I said, then stepped toward the stairs. "I might have other plans," I added over my shoulder as I climbed the stairs.

"You'll get used to it. And I told you before, plans change," Dom said.

"Pfft," was my reply as I reached the landing, then stomped to my room at Dom's chuckle.

"Maybe I'm the one who needs some medication or therapy. Since instead of putting down my foot about him telling me what to do, I'm doing it. No questions asked," I said while I moved around my bedroom doing what the man said to do. After I change into jeans, pulled my boots on, then yanked the sweatshirt over my head, I headed back downstairs.

"Sounded like you were having a pleasant conversation with yourself," Dom said with a smirk on his face.

"Oh, kiss my ass, Dom," I said, in defense of the fact he overheard me ranting.

"Maybe later. Let's go," he commented and grabbed my jacket off the back of the chair before he opened the door and waited for me to go out first.

While upstairs, I stuck cash in one jean pocket, cell phone in the pocket of my sweatshirt, and after I locked my front door, I shoved my keys in another pocket. Then Dom led me to his bike.

"Umm...would now be a good time to tell you I've never ridden on a motorcycle," I said and bit my lip, looking at the two-wheeled machine.

"No problem." Dom reached in the bag on the side of his bike and pulled out a helmet and handed to me, then placed my jacket inside. After he grabbed his helmet off the seat, he helped with mine, snapping the strap on the side after placing it under my chin. Once he was on the bike, he patted the seat behind him. "Get on."

I awkwardly did as he had done and placed my feet on the bars Dom kicked out on each side.

"Now, wrap your arms around me and hold on. Only thing you gotta do is go with the bike. Other than that, enjoy. Ready?"

"Yes," I answered, took a deep breath, and wrapped my arms around Dom's waist. He waited for me to get settled, then cranked the bike. The sound of the pipes was loud, which I'd heard motorcycles before just never rode on one. But when he backed the bike out of the driveway to the street, then kicked it in gear, I held on a little tighter because, good grief, the vibration was something I hadn't expected.

We rode on main street before heading out of town, and I couldn't stop looking around. It was definitely a different view than being inside a car. As we came upon the building where I took yoga classes and where the Black Hawk MC gym was, I saw Sami and Luna with their men along with others on the sidewalk. Dom slowed enough to throw up his hand as we passed by. The group waved, but all I could do was smile. No way was I letting go of Dom.

When we reached the outskirts of town, Dom patted my leg, then sped up. The road had more and more curves the farther we got away from town.

"Relax, River," Dom yelled over the sound of the bike. With the helmet on, his voice was muffled and caused me to press against his back.

"I'm not sure I can," I said close to his ear. The position made it easier, and I heard Dom chuckle.

"By the time this ride is over, you'll wonder how you've gone without ever riding on a bike."

"If you say so."

"You're doing great, baby. You're leaning with me, and the bike like you've always ridden behind me," Dom said as he removed one hand from the handlebar and squeezed my calf.

"Should you be doing that?" I asked and felt his body shaking. "Are you laughing at me? It isn't funny. You should keep your hands on the bars."

"Whatever you want. You ready for a pit stop?"

"Sure," I said and noticed as I looked around that we seemed to be heading into civilization again as we passed by a few spaced out houses and an occasional building.

We rode a few more miles when Dom slowed and pulled off the road into the lot of a gas station. Next door to it sat an aged building that was evidently a restaurant, if the sign hanging on the front of it was correct. He pulled up to the pump and shut the bike off.

"You can let go now, River," Dom said, and patted my arms that were still wrapped around his waist.

"Sorry," I said and released him.

"Hold on to my shoulders and slide off until your one foot is on the ground, then swing your other leg over. Make sure you keep hold of me until you get your legs under you. You're going to be a bit stiff at first."

I did as he said, and when both my feet were on the ground, I groaned.

"Oh my God, I can't feel my legs or my butt," I said while I pulled off the helmet.

Dom smiled, pulled his own helmet off, and hook it on one handle. He then got off the bike with an ease that had to come from years of riding.

"Normal for first-timers. Once you walk around, it will work itself out. I'm just going to top off my tank, then we'll go to the restaurant and have lunch. It doesn't look like much, but the food is excellent. Brothers and I found this place when we were out riding one time," Dom said as he started filling his gas tank, and I stood off to the side.

"It's already lunchtime?" I asked and looked at my watch.

"We've been riding for a couple of hours."

"Wow, it didn't feel like we'd been gone that long. I guess with all the scenery to look at, you don't think about how much time you've been riding."

"No, you don't. Well... unless you get stuck in the rain, then you either tough it out or look for a place to get out of it and hope it blows over."

It didn't take long for the tank to fill, and Dom was ready to move the bike. I looked at the bike, then over to the other building. It wasn't that far away.

"I'll meet you over there. Maybe walking will bring the feeling in my butt cheeks back. Besides, it will be quicker than me getting back on and off again."

I hadn't expected it and was surprised when Dom leaned in and kissed my forehead.

"Meet you there," he said and mounted the bike.

I stood there a second before I turned and started toward the restaurant. For an out of the way place, there were quite a few vehicles in the parking lot. So, either other people passing by were taking a chance on the place, or the logical answer was the foliage probably hid homes from view with its thickness, and this was one of the local dives.

By the time I reached the entrance, Dom was backed into a spot in the front and was getting off his bike.

Once inside, we were seated and given menus to look at while the older lady went to retrieve our drinks. The outside wasn't in the best of shape, and though the inside was old, it was clean. Plus, if the aroma in the air was a sign, the food would be good.

The waitress was back and after she set the drinks down; she pulled a pad out of her apron. "What can I get you?"

I told her what I wanted and handed her the menu. Then Dom followed suit. When she left to place our orders, I looked at Dom.

"Tell me about your club?" I asked before he had the time to speak. I wasn't ready to answer questions about myself. Not because I had anything to hide. I hadn't lived a very exciting life. But from the small amount my dad had shared with me on the Black Hawk MC, Dom and the others had.

Chapter Nine

Jag

Stopping had been more for me than for River. I needed a break from having her essentially wrapped around me. The woman was oblivious to the effect she had on me. With her thighs snuggly encasing my hips, her chest pressed into my back, and her arms wrapped tightly at my waist, I felt every ounce of her heat through my clothing. A couple of hours of that and my concentration was gone.

I might have mentioned that I wanted to go slow with her, but it wasn't going to happen. Not after speaking with her dad, and definitely not after tasting her. Any doubt I had of what I wanted went away with a vision of River naked and wrapped around me, and not on a bike. Well...at least not right now.

"Tell me about your club?"

River's question shook me out of my head, and I realized I was staring at her while I dealt with my thoughts. I wanted to get her to open up to me, but she beat me to the punch.

"Do you know anything about MCs?" I asked.

"Other than what my dad told me after I'd seen a few men around town with vests on."

"Which was...?" I questioned and raised my brow.

"Mainly how the club came to be in Shades Valley. At first, there may or may not have been some illegal activity going on with the club, but with no tangible proof, means there are no court records to prove otherwise. He told me you and the others who make up the leadership... and I have to say, I'm not sure I understand that part... were raised by your single dads. No details on why. The club does a lot for the community, which has helped with the town's overall acceptance of the club. Really, his information was basic.

"So, this might make me sound naïve, even stupid to ask, but I assume your club isn't anything like what they depicted in SOA? I binged watched the series on *Netflix* since I've had free time. I'll admit it hooked me and I can't wait to catch the spinoff MC show. There are tons of books out with the same theme. I've even purchased a few and they bring romance books to a new level. And what I noticed seeing the men in your club, watching SOA, and the books, the common denominator is hot gu—" River abruptly stopped talking, and her face grew flushed.

I grinned. "You think the men in my club are hot?" I teased. The waitress brought our food, which gave River a break in answering, but no way would I let that statement drop.

Once the waitress walked away, River immediately started in on her food. I'd play along for a bit, so I picked up my burger and started eating, too. Since I missed breakfast, I plowed through my food before River was halfway through hers.

"While you finish, I'll tell you what I can about the club, or most clubs in general. Don't believe everything you read or watch on television about MCs. Are there some that deal in illegal things, sure, but they aren't the norm. However, they still follow common club rules. No MC deals well with betrayal of any type. It's a brotherhood where loyalty is primary. Everyone inside the club is family until they do something that would make them not be any longer. Stroker, Flyboy, Preacher, Cutter, Cruz, and Romeo formed Black Hawk. They served in the military together and were the original leadership until me, Crusher, Flirt, Coast, Devil, and Speed came home. We've been back a few months for a while. Speed was the last to make it home. Once he arrived, our dads stepped down and turned the club over to us. Now we are the leadership. Crusher is President, I'm the Vice President, Devil is the Secretary, Coast and Speed are Enforcers, and Flirt is the Treasurer.

"The club owns several businesses. A club member runs each, and most of the employees are members, too. We are pretty self-sufficient. TV is great for entertainment, but..." I shrugged.

River finished with her food, wiped her mouth and hands, then placed her napkin on the table.

"I think there is more to the club."

"Some things you don't need to know."

"Is this where you say the women aren't privy to the inner decisions and activities of the club?" River asked, and I saw amusement in her eyes.

"Yes."

"Seriously, you mean the men in the club keep things from their SOs or wives? That sounds a bit archaic," she stated, the amusement in her eyes gone as she glared at me.

"Sometimes knowing less is better." My lips twitched at her glare. "Enough on my club. Let's get out of here. I want to take you somewhere else. Then it's my turn, and you can tell me about yourself."

"Hey, you didn't tell me anything about yourself," River commented and slid out of the booth. When she pulled cash from her pocket, I lifted a brow. "What? I want to pay for my food."

"Not happening when you are with me, so put your money away." I slid several bills into the folder the waitress left when she'd brought our food. It was enough to cover our meal and a nice tip for the waitress.

"You're bossy."

"Yes, I am, and hot by your admission," I replied, chuckled as I stood, then placed my hand on the small of her back to lead her out.

"I'm surprised the bike doesn't tip over from your swollen head," River mumbled as we reached the bike.

"Since both my heads are swollen, it balances out." I grabbed the helmets and handed one to her.

"I can't believe you said that!"

"You brought it up, literally." I winked, then leaned in before giving her a quick peck on the lips. She slammed the face shield down, and I smirked. "Going to jump on the highway a couple miles up the road. The place I want to show you isn't far from Shades Valley."

River nodded, and I mounted my bike. Once she was on and wrapped around me again, I started the bike and pulled out.

When we got on the highway, and I increased the bike's speed, she tightened her arms around my waist. As we cruised down the highway, I rested a hand on one of hers and rubbed it with my thumb. We fit, she fit. I briefly wondered how long it would take me to convince her of the same thing.

Taking the highway cut the time and a little over an hour later, I was taking the exit we needed. It was another spot the others and I found while out riding. Only locals knew of the spot unless someone accidentally came across it, which meant they were lost. Getting to it, the scenery was thick with trees and foliage blocking out everything until you reached the one spot that let you know what all it was hiding. We rode through the curve, and I slowed and eased off the road onto the soft and gravelly ground.

"Oh...my...God," River said. I stopped the bike at one of the few picnic tables that were there. It was the first time I stopped there and no one else was around.

River got off the bike without looking away from the sight. Once I was off, I grabbed her hand and walked her to the guardrail that kept you away from the drop-off.

"I thought you might like it," I said and squeezed her hand.

"It is beautiful. I know the ocean is farther than it looks. But it's like the mountains are teasing you with what is on the other side of them." The awe in her voice made me smile.

"Whoa," I said as she stepped over the rail. "I know there's a good bit of grassy area there, but you never know if the cliff's edge might slide. You definitely don't want to fall into the ravine."

"I wonder if you could follow the ravine to the ocean."

"That would be one long trek. Not sure it even runs that far."

River sat on the rail, and I straddled it beside her and wrapped my arms around her waist.

"I don't remember much about living here. I was almost five when my mom and I left. But since I've moved back, the beauty of the area and especially this, just makes me more confused on why my mother left. Why would anyone leave here and move to an overpopulated area where to go anywhere you have to fight traffic?"

"That was the one thing I hated when I lived in the DC area. I learned a lot of back ways to avoid I95. Rush hour never failed to turn into a parking lot. Especially if you were in a hurry to be somewhere."

"You didn't want to stay in the military?"

"Maybe at some point the thought entered my mind, but if it did, it didn't stay long. I knew I would come back here. It's home."

"Why an attorney?"

"The law was interesting to me. I wanted to go to college while the others decided they wanted to see more than where we grew up. My plan was to get my law degree and come home and be the MC's attorney. I was on track for that, too. Then one visit when we were all home at the same time, hearing them discuss what they'd done and their experiences, I thought what the hell. I went back to school and visited the local Navy recruiting station. So when the time came to graduate law school, I was committed to the Navy. With a six years commitment, they covered my loans. Now I'm the club's VP and attorney and can help my club with everything legal wise and I don't have astronomical debt hanging over my head. What about you? Sami mentioned you were going to be Ally's teacher. Did you always want to be a teacher?" I asked, and before she answered, she straddled the rail, then leaned backed on me. "Come on, let's move to the picnic table. It will be more comfortable."

I helped her up and moved us to the table. She sat on top of the table, and I went to the bike and grabbed the couple of bottles of water that I threw in before I left the house. They'd be a little warm, but at least it was wet. When I offered her one, she shook her head, and I set them down in reach, then joined her on the table, putting my arm around her and pulling her into my side. It surprised me when she laid her head against my shoulder.

"So, did you always want to be a teacher?" I asked again.

"Yes. I used to play in my room with my stuffed animals as my students."

"Did you teach in Connecticut?"

"I didn't get the chance to. After I graduated from college, I married, and Thomas wanted to start a family immediately. Which now I'm grateful I finished my degree."

"Why wouldn't you have finished?" I looked down to see her face when she chuckled and in a tone that had nothing to do with humor and everything to do with bitterness.

"You'd have to know my mother. She didn't understand why I wanted to go to college in the first place. My stepdad is a partner in the same law firm as Thomas's dad. We grew up around each other. Thomas is four years older and for as long as I could remember, my mother saw him and I getting together. I think she thought, why bother? If he would eventually join the same law firm, I wouldn't have to work. I could spend my time helping build his clientele by hosting parties and volunteering for charities run by high profiled people. After I told her I would be done with college around the time Thomas graduated law school, she back off some. I mean, she was discussing this as if

Thomas had already proposed, which he hadn't. I was just getting ready to turn eighteen."

I listened as River told me some things her dad had already shared. I noticed the more she talked about her mother, the more hurt that came into her voice.

"I don't know why I still let the things she's done influence me. It's over. I'm here, and I refuse to buckle to her way anymore." She tilted her head to look up at me. "And I'm sorry for putting a damper on such a lovely day with you by talking about my mother and ex. Boy, aren't I a prize to take on a date?"

I wanted to ask what happened with her and the ex, but it wasn't the time. Instead, I grinned and leaned in. This kiss was soft and slow, and it was the first time I remember ever wanting to show a woman gentleness. Hard, fast, and explosive was how I liked it. But with River, I took my time enjoying her taste. When she shivered as the wind blew, I broke our kiss.

"Let me get your jacket." I moved to get off the table.

"You're a dangerous man, Dom."

I frowned as I stood in front of her. "What makes you think so?"

"Because you listen, you're attentive to what's happening around you, and you're very easy to talk to. I bet you are one damn talented attorney."

"And hot." She laughed as I wanted her to.

"And incorrigible."

I chuckled and looked at my watch. "If we leave now, we'll get into town in time that I could take you to dinner."

"How do you feel about cold chicken and potato salad?"

"Homemade potato salad?" I asked with a raised eyebrow.

"What other kind is there?"

"And where would we be eating this food?" I asked with a grin. I knew she was talking about her house, but I wanted her to say it.

"If you don't mind, we can go to my house. Where, I not only have those items, but half an apple pie as well. Plus, I have a nice plush couch to sit on. I think my tushy deserves it."

"Well, we can't have your *tushy* sore, so your house it is," I said and grabbed her around her waist and lifted her off the table. In no time, we were back on my bike and headed to Shades Valley.

"That was great, River. Thank you." I rose with my empty plate and reached for River's.

"I got it." She stood, and as we walked, she flinched.

"Stiffening up?" I asked and took the plate before she dropped it.

"I don't know how you ride all the time. My God, my butt hurts and the inside of my thighs gives me an idea of what it's like to ride a horse. I'd bet money that's where the saying 'save a horse, ride a cowboy' comes from. Heck, it would have to feel better. I'm going to start saying 'save a bike, ride a biker.'" She abruptly stopped and looked at me.

My lips twitched as I watched the pink form on her cheeks when she realized what she said.

"Hmm... I could get on board with that," I commented and set the plates in the sink. "But not tonight. I'm going to head home so you can soak..." I walked to her and wrapped my arms around her, "this fine ass." I placed my hands on her ass and started massaging.

River leaned her forehead on my chest and slipped her arms around my waist. I felt myself begin to harden when she moaned.

"Oh my God, that feels good," she whispered into my chest.

"Ah, sweetheart, you'll get used to it the more you ride. I'll just have to make a habit of taking you out regularly, so you can get adjusted to it. Now kiss me, then you can go take a hot bath."

"Bossy," she mumbled, but raised her head and did as I asked. I kissed her until we both were breathless, then turned us toward the front door.

"Lock up, and I'll see you sometime tomorrow." I kissed her forehead and opened the door.

"I don't know what time I'll be home. I'm going shopping with Sami, Carly, Luna, and Bailey."

"Well, you girls stay out of trouble, and I'll come by later in the day. Got a few things to take care of tomorrow, anyway." I stepped out on the stoop. "Don't forget to lock the door."

"I won't," she answered, and I pulled the door shut and waited until I heard the locks engage before I headed to my bike.

On the ride home, I thought about how the day had gone. The time with River and getting to know her was enjoyable. She might have started out a little tense when we headed out, but by the time we left the lookout place, she was relaxed.

I threw my hand up at Lock as I slowed going through the gate at Black Hawk. Once I was in my house, I was already looking forward to spending time with River again. Tomorrow couldn't come soon enough.

Chapter Ten

River

Dressed and ready to go, I walked out of the house and locked the door when the women pulled into my driveway. As I reached the SUV, the back door on the passenger side opened, and Bailey slid to the middle to make room for me. We exchanged hellos and after I shut the door, Carly, who was in the driver's seat, backed out of the driveway and we were on our way.

"You okay with the mall, River?" Sami asked from the passenger seat as she looked through the space between the seats.

"The mall would be good. They have a craft store, right? This morning I was thinking I would hit the store and see what I could find to decorate my classroom."

"Oh yeah, I love that store. I find the most unique things in there to make ornaments with," Bailey said, and I nodded.

"No, not another crafty person," Luna said. "I guess you crochet, too?"

"Not me. My crafting skills only reach to items that are easy for children to work with," I said.

"I could teach you. It's easy. This one," Bailey pointed her thumb in Luna's direction, "thinks it's a waste of time. I use it for its calming effect."

"I use Brax for that," Luna said.

"Sometimes I need to relax when Devil isn't home," Bailey said, and Luna lifted a brow as she looked at Bailey.

"Oh, I just use the toys in my nightstand drawer," Luna replied. Carly and Sami laughed, and Bailey patted my back when I choked.

"Luna, you are going to give River the wrong impression. She's going to think all we talk about is sex," Bailey chastised.

"From what I know, there are three of you that show you do more than talk," I said, and Luna, Bailey, along with Sami, who once again looked between the seats, stared at me with wide eyes. It startled me when Carly hit the steering wheel with her hand and started laughing.

"That was awesome. Give it up, sister," Carly said and stretched her right arm between the seats with her hand balled up into a fist. I leaned forward and bumped my fist against hers.

It was that easy to make friends, and I knew these women would become mine. With what amounted to breaking the ice, we talked about everything from which business to stay clear of in town because their prices were high, to how each woman had met and ended up with her man. I learned Luna and Ghost had grown up next door together and met up again after Ghost lost his wife and child, then came to Shades Valley to heal. Luna had been with the Ops Warriors in San Diego. Talk about fate bringing two people back together.

Bailey and Devil had been high school sweethearts, then when he had come home from the military, pulled his head out of his ass—her words not mine—they rekindled the love they still had for each other.

Carly and Sami were associated with the Haven MC, a club Sami's dad ran as President. I was shocked to learn how Carly and Speed had found out they were actually brother and sister and that Sami had slept with Speed not even knowing who he was, and he did not know he had fathered a child until he returned from the military and accidentally ran into Ally at the grocery store.

Sami told the story about how Carly and Crusher met, and I smiled when she said that he patiently outlasted her prickly friend.

They shared funny stories about Ally and Neely. I never laughed so much in my life. I wiped under my eyes and was glad I used the waterproof mascara, or I would have it smeared across my face.

"So, are you going to tell us how yesterday went with Jag?" Luna asked, and I glanced over at her.

"Why would you think I spent the day with Dom?" I asked.

"Because I was at the gym helping Ghost load the computer programs they will need when Coast came in and said Jag was spending the day with you if anyone needed him. And duh, you were riding on the back of his bike when he rode past."

"Oh, yeah. It was nice," I answered Luna's original question.

"Just nice?" Sami asked.

"Well..." I didn't get to finish when Luna cut me off.

"Did you two douse some of those flames?" Luna inquired.

"Luna!" Bailey chastised.

"Like none of you are curious. The man has been grouchy since I've known him. When he came back into the bar the other day, after he followed River out, it was like he had a personality change. I mean, you guys told me he wasn't himself, but I'd never seen him act any other way. And the first time I saw River and Jag interact was in front of Yoga Sensual, and let me tell ya, I'm surprised Ghost and I didn't have to hose the two of them down. As they talked to each other sparks were flying off them," Luna commented and looked at the others as if to see if either of them would dispute her.

"Well, his bike was in front of his place this morning, so I'm going to answer and say they didn't do the deed.

Because not that I know anything about Jag's umm... prowess, but if he's anything like Crusher, no way would he have been home," Carly spoke up as she continued to watch the road.

"River, you don't have to tell them anything other than to mind their own business. But they are nosey and will continue to hound you," Sami said, and Bailey agreed.

"Aren't you two the queens of what is polite?" Carly said.

"Better than the queen of no tact!" Sami shot back. I watched as the two women went back and forth with insults.

"Please, have pity for us. Those two can keep that up for hours, and if you at least tell us what non-getting-naked activities the two of you did, it will shut them up," Luna said, and I laughed at her pout and the puppy dog eyes Bailey turned on me for added effect.

"Fine," I said, rolled my eyes, and began sharing how Dom and I shared the day. When I finished, we were pulling into a parking space at one end of the mall.

"Aww," all four women said.

"I didn't know any of them knew how to be romantic," Carly said, then added. "They are more like I imagine a caveman to be romantic. Hit you over the head, kill something for you to eat, then kiss you until you give in."

I laughed with the others as we looked to make sure nothing was coming as we crossed to the sidewalk in front of the mall entrance. We only had to wait until the one car that was close passed. When we reached the sidewalk, Carly was still watching the car that had driven by.

"What's up?" Sami asked.

"Just weird. That car looked like the same one parked on the street across from Sue's house," Carly said, and frowned.

"Are you getting back into deputy mode?" Bailey asked.

"There are hundreds of those cars around, but it is strange because that one has the same scuff mark over the passenger side rear tire well. Like they got too close to something and scraped the side," Carly mused, then turned and pulled the mall door open.

"Well, they're gone now. What do think about going down one side of the mall, then we can go to the food court and have lunch before hitting the other side?" Luna said as the five of us walked inside.

"Good grief, can't go anywhere with you guys if you aren't thinking of food," Carly said and shook her head.

"Hey, eating for three," Luna answered.

"I'm not eating for three, but I am thrilled to eat, and have it stay down," Sami added.

"I stay hungry. I'm going to weigh three hundred pounds before this pregnancy is over," Bailey commented.

Carly hooked her arm through mine. "Let's get them waddling along, River, because I don't think they'll wait for us to reach the food court. They will stop at every food spot on the way. Cookies, pretzels, and then drinks, which brings us to locating the nearest restroom." I chuckled when Luna, Sami, and Bailey flipped Carly as they passed us.

I closed the door, set my shopping bags in the corner of the living room, then fell back onto the couch and sighed. Even though I was tired, I was looking forward to seeing Dom. I caught myself throughout the day wondering what he was doing.

The shopping trip had been long, but I enjoyed every minute with the women. When they dropped me off, we made plans to get together soon. We'd have to wait for Carly, who was starting back to work tomorrow, and Bailey to be off. Luna filled in at a couple of the club's businesses when they needed her, and she handled the books for Ghost and Dare's construction company that had just gotten up and running. I looked forward to spending more time with them.

I was proud of only having a moment of sadness today. We'd stopped in the baby store to look around. Luckily, the women were too busy to see the couple of tears that slipped out when I picked up a tiny outfit. I let myself have the moment, then took a deep breath, wiped away the wetness, and put the outfit back down. Maybe one day, it wouldn't hurt to think about what I would never have. I'd have to be content spoiling other people's children.

Who knows, when I got over not being able to have my own, adoption was always an option. There were plenty of children in the world that needed someone to love them.

The ringing of my cell phone had me up and moving to the kitchen. I'd forgotten I'd left it charging on the counter when I left the house.

Looking at the screen, I inwardly groaned when I saw my mother's number. I debated answering, but manners had me swiping the screen.

"Hello, Mother," I said in greeting.

"River," was her reply because it's so hard to ask how someone is doing.

"How is everything with you and Alfred?" I walked around the kitchen, fixed a glass of tea, then opened the back door. I stood in front of the screen door, enjoying the breeze that was blowing into the house.

"That sounds lovely, Mother," I said at the appropriate time during the conversation. I knew she would get to why she was calling eventually because there was always a reason. My mother was not a call to chit-chat woman.

I didn't know how long I was on the phone—I mean how many fundraisers can one woman chair—then she switched to how Alfred always ignored her when she wanted to update something in their house—on and on with things I'd never had an interest in.

When she finally got around to the point of her call, I had to ask her to repeat what she said because I zoned out on the stool I pulled out and sat on. No sense being uncomfortable while I listened.

"Sorry, Mother, can you repeat that?" I asked, and her sigh came across the airways as clear as if she sat beside me.

"I said I've done what you asked and haven't given your new number to Thomas, but he wants to talk to you, River. I don't know what it would hurt to listen to the man.

He told Alfred that he knows he messed up, but he still loves you."

"Mother, that is one of the great things about being divorced. I have no obligation to listen."

"Don't get smart with me. I've not said anything to you about how the divorce has affected Alfred and me. We can't go to social events or parties without the whispers and looks. Thomas Sr. is upset, too."

"So... you've all sat around and discussed *my* divorce?" I asked, closed my eyes and pinched my nose.

"Well, yes, his son is distraught. Why wouldn't he want to help him?"

"Like you want to help me?"

"Yes!"

"And what are you going to do to help?" Nothing was ever going to change our relationship. When would I learn and just move on?

"I'm trying to tell you. Call Thomas or let me give him your number. You pushed for a speedy divorce by telling him you would let every one of his clients and friends at the country club know what he'd done unless he signed the papers. You forced his hand. He didn't want a divorce. He feels his chance of any type of reconciliation is getting slimmer by the day. You can't be happy there, River. I mean, the area is pretty, don't get me wrong, but that is what vacations are for. And if you want to teach so bad, why don't you apply at one of the private schools here? At least you would know the students are from upper middle class to the substantially wealthy in the area. Their parents are pillars in the community."

I rubbed the back of my neck. The tension was there, and I felt the beginning of a headache.

"So, I'll give Thomas your number, and the two of you can work on reconciling."

"No, Mother. If you give him my number, I will change it again and I won't give it to you either." The pause was long enough that I thought she might have hung up.

"Thomas was right, you are seeing some biker. Is he part of the club that I remember being around the area? I mean really, River, you've been given every opportunity. If you are adamant about not going back to Thomas, you could at least move up in class. Instead of lowering yourself. I guess I should have expected as much with you being around your father."

"Mother, how does Thomas know anything about me?" I asked through clenched teeth.

"So, it is true?"

"Mother!"

"Don't you raise your voice to me! He wanted to make sure you were okay there. He hired a private investigator. The man reported back to him today and when Thomas told me, I called you because I couldn't believe you would do something like that. I thought the man must have made a mistake. Now, I see you've made a fool out of me once again! How could you?"

To say I had enough would be an understatement. The heat on my face was a sign that my blood pressure was topping off. It was time to release some of the pressure, along with years of wondering why the woman who was supposed to love me unconditionally didn't. I was done.

"Since you seem to be chatty with Thomas, you can relay anything I'm going to say that you feel he needs to know. The PI better go away, or I will have Thomas served at the firm with a restraining order. And we know how *that* will go over. As far as seeing a biker, he is more a man than Thomas will ever be. *That club*, as you called it. The people I have met who are associated with it have been nice, accepting, and not once judgmental of me. Unlike my mother! My father doesn't know how lucky he is that you divorced him. My only regret is when I got of age, I didn't demand to live with him.

"I am his daughter and proud of it. But I am not proud to be yours. Are you listening, Mother?"

"I will not listen anymore. I'm going to hang up and let you think about what you've said and wait for your apology.

"Oh no, Mother. You are going to want to stay on the line and hear it all because there will be no apology, ever. Because I am done. Do you hear me? D.O.N.E. I will not get back with Thomas. He CHEATED and, by cheating, put himself in a situation of his own making. When I confronted him about it, he blamed me for his faults. And you, Mother, can keep your high society ass where it is—don't call me, don't write me, don't text me—I will let you know if I want to resume our relationship. And so help me, if you call my dad and say one word to him, there will never be a chance of resuming our relationship.

"But before *I* hang up, I will thank you for one thing—I have found who I was always supposed to be. I've looked for her for years. Your call has set her free. Enjoy your life, Mother, because I plan to enjoy mine." After I disconnected the call, I took several deep breaths and put my head on my arms. I heard the screen door and didn't bother to look, I knew it was Dom. I only briefly wondered how much he heard.

"Let's go. You need to get out of here and clear your head. We'll go for a ride, then you are coming to my house," he said and laid a hand on my back and rubbed.

No hounding me about what was going on. Just giving me support. I swiveled the stool and stood.

"I think I'd like that," I said, then closed the door and locked it. Dom never said a word. He only grabbed my keys as we walked past the table beside the couch. Once the front door was locked, we got on his bike, and I wrapped myself around him and we were off. As we rode, I laid my head on his back and let his heartbeat release the last of my tension, guilt, and hurt.

Chapter Eleven

Jag

I knocked on River's front door and waited, but instead of hearing her moving toward the door, I heard her yelling at someone. I tried the knob and when it didn't turn; I headed around back. When I reached for the screen door and saw her sitting on the stool, her back to the door, yelling into her cell, I stopped. It didn't take long for me to figure out her mother was on the other end. The conversation didn't sound as if it was going well.

Overhearing River with her mom, and learning what her douchebag ex-husband had done, explained most of River's insecurities and why she used verbal defenses to cover them. To have River then stray—what an idiot. It proved he never deserved her.

With her on the back of my bike, we rode in silence for an hour before I turned into Black Hawk. Everything in me wanted to prove to her she was a desirable woman, and it was the prick's failure in not seeing what he had. It had nothing to do with her. I also didn't miss from the conversation that her mother was more interested in the ramifications of what the divorce had done to her social appearance than the reason it had taken place.

All I knew was my thoughts were filled with River. And I only needed to remember the heat of her body pressed to mine, and I was beyond worked up. I needed to show her, feel her in my arms while she curled around me in my bed. Somewhere in the back of my mind, I knew I had to slow down so not to frighten her. But by the time we were off the bike and entering my house and I took a good look at her, nothing else mattered.

The door closed when I pushed River back against it and started kissing her. I only broke the kiss long enough to pull her jacket down her shoulders and pull her shirt over her head. Then placed my lips back on hers. If she had any doubt about what was going to take place, she didn't voice it. Her bra followed next, and then I unfastened her pants. They were more of an issue because I would have to break the kiss to get them pushed down. Deciding, I broke the kiss, kneeled, and removed her shoes. Every item tossed to the side as I yanked until her pants were down. Briefly, I glanced at the thong she wore, but in my rush to have her naked before me, I slid them off to join her other clothing. As I stood, I took her body in. There was something to be said about being completely dressed while she was bare.

"Sweetheart, you are as close to perfection as a woman can get," I praised, my voice sounding hoarse to my own ears.

She reached up and ran her fingers through my hair and closed the space between us. River raised on tiptoes until our lips met. She started the kiss, but I took over and without pretense, I devoured her. It was the only word to describe how I demanded and thoroughly dominated the kiss. Neither of us could get enough. Our tongues dueled, and I ran my hands down River's sides, resting them on her hips. Goosebumps broke out on her skin from the trail of my hands.

I moved my hands behind her and grabbed the cheeks of her ass, then squeezed and caressed. When I lifted her up, she wrapped her legs around my waist, bringing her bare pussy in contact with the material of my jeans.

She rubbed against me, and my cock throbbed. I shifted to gain a better grip on her legs, and the move placed her directly over my shaft. River moaned as I rolled my hips. I looked into her eyes and saw desire in her green eyes.

My nostrils flared, and I adjusted my grip and turned toward the stairs. In my room, I laid River on the bed and worked on removing my clothing. I grabbed a condom from the nightstand, tore it open, and rolled it on. Joining her on the bed, I shifted until I laid between her legs and rested my upper body weight on my forearms.

"Please, Dominic."

I stared into River's eyes. My whole first name rolling from between her lips had me losing the last of my control. I reached between us, felt the wetness of River's desire for me. I wanted to take my time, worship her body, but it would have to wait. This time was going to be pure need—the need to feel her surrounding me. I slammed home in one thrust. River's back arched and her head bent back onto the pillow while I stilled to let her adjust to my size.

When the grip of her pussy on my dick loosened, I moved. I pulled out and thrusted back in. Relentlessly I worked to reach my peak as I was to provide her with more pleasure than any man would give to her.

River's hips rose to meet mine, the pace I set brutal, but she had no problem keeping up.

"Oh God, I've never felt like this," River got out between pants. Heavy breathing and the slapping of skin on skin sounded in the room.

I wasn't going to last long, but I wanted to prolong her release and mine, so I gritted my teeth and willed myself to stop. River moaned her displeasure, and I smiled as I lowered my head to her chest. Still seated deep inside her, I flicked one hard nipple with my tongue, then moved to the other and did the same.

She wiggled beneath me and brought her hand between us until it rested on her clit. Guess she figured if I wasn't going to get her off, she'd do it herself.

She was wrong.

"Nuh uh." I raised until I rested on my knees and grabbed both her wrists and stretched her arms above her head. "I'll get you off my way. But if you move those hands, I will get myself off and leave you hanging on the edge. Then I will turn you over my knees and spank your ass until it is so red, you'll see and feel my handprint for a week."

"You're an asshole. Get off me and take me home. You probably can't get the job done, and that's why you're stalling." River's eyes were wide, and her breathing had picked up, which told me she enjoyed razzing me. And the tone to her voice had me swelling more, almost to the bursting point.

Christ, I had to be one sick bastard to be turned on, but I could live with it.

"Ah, sweetheart, your mouth is saying one thing, but the quivering of your pussy around my dick tells me something different. You like what I'm doing to you, don't you?"

"Yes!" I watched her face redden under my stare until she turned her head away. I used one of my hands to hold her wrists while I moved the other to turn her face back to mine.

"Don't ever hide from me, River. Ever. It should never embarrass you to ask for what you want. Sex should be enjoyable for both parties. Exhilarating if the ones involved are open with their needs. I'll give you what you need and take everything I want. If I don't do something you want, then tell me."

She watched me closely, and if I had seen one drop of uncertainty in her eyes, I would have stopped, but none was there. It was as if her eyes held a challenge in their depths.

Yet it didn't keep her from trying to hide whatever feelings were there.

"I'm not sure I ca—" Her words were cut off when, in a swift move, I let go of her wrists, pulled out, and flipped her onto her stomach.

I'd had enough of her head fighting with her body. Her ex had done a helluva job on her. So instead of arguing, I would just show her. I would punch that bastard in the face if he ever were in front of me.

Once I had her positioned on her knees with her cheek pressed into the mattress, I used my own knees to spread her legs wide, then plunged back in. I gritted my teeth as I held her hips and tried to give her a minute to catch the breath my move had taken from her. When she inadvertently pushed back, I took it as a sign to move. She wouldn't be able to argue with me if she was screaming my name. And she would, several times before I was finished with her.

As I worked in and out of her, I moved my hands from her hips and rubbed the cheeks of her ass. The moan she released every time I bottomed out told me she was enjoying what we were doing.

"Faster, Dom. I need more."

I inwardly grinned at her breathlessly spoken words. She wanted to hide, but underneath was a woman who could match any man's needs and have him the one begging for more. It was just getting her to acknowledge her wants and desires. And if I had to fuck her from sundown to sunrise, and in every position I could think of, I would get River to do just that.

My balls drew up, and I knew I had held off as long as I could, but I wanted her to go over with me. Sliding some of her wetness to her back hole, I massaged the puckered skin. At first, she whimpered, and I almost stopped until she pushed back, causing my thumb to breach the tiny hole. The deep groan and the shiver that went through her body had me pushing the digit in and out, mimicking the movement of my cock.

"That's it, River. Give me everything you got, baby. We'll go over together. Going to take this hole, too, but not today. We'll work up to that." Her body quivered, but she didn't go over. "As tight as you are, I'm sure your ass will choke my cock, but it'll be so good that neither of us will resist. Think you'd like that? The bite of pain before the pleasure consumes you."

"Shut up, Dom, and make me come!" she yelled, and I reached around her with my free hand and pinched her clit none too gently. When her walls clamped down around me, I pinched her clit again. The second time had the same result, but the thrusting in until the head of my cock touched her cervix, and my thumb slid all the way into her ass, brought out the deepest groan yet from her. My body was shaking, and my dick was pulsing with the need to spill everything I had in me.

Yeah, she was a dream in bed. And she was going to be mine. She just didn't know it yet.

The thought of all the things I wanted to do to her had me bending over her and slamming into the hilt with each thrust of my hips. I left my thumb buried in her back hole, but I moved my hand from her clit to her breasts and twisted her nipple between the thumb and forefinger until my name poured from her lips.

Beads of sweat ran down the sides of my face and moisture formed between us from the heat of our skin.

"Dominic!" The scream was loud and echoed off the walls, and as River spasmed around me, I went over the edge with her.

The force of my release brought black spots behind my eyes. When I finished, and every drop had been drained until I softened enough to slip from her heat, I collapsed beside her.

"I think I'm going to like your way." I smiled at the exhaustion in her voice.

"Give me a few minutes, and I'll show you how much more there is." I sat up to dispose of the condom and froze as I noticed the tear. "Shit."

"Hmm."

"I'm sorry, River. The condom broke," I said and touched her hip.

"Don't worry, it won't be a problem," she said, her voice muffled as she snuggled her face into the pillow and sighed.

"No problem? Don't worry. Are you on the pill?" I asked and got no reply. She was asleep.

I stood, walked into the bathroom, disposed of the condom, and washed my hands. I'd ask her later about birth control. It wasn't the first time I ever had a condom break, but when it happened on those few occasions, panic kicked in. It wasn't there this time, which should have sent me into a different type of panic. I breathed deep, wiped my hands down my face as a breathed out. Screw it, I'd analyze shit later. I needed sleep.

Walking back into the bedroom, I climbed into bed beside River. She groaned, and I wrapped my arms around her and pulled her into the curve of my body. She fit as if she belonged there.

The ringing of my cell had me opening my eyes. And the light coming through the blinds let me know it was morning. River stretched and mumbled something incoherent as I worked my arm from under her, then reached for the phone on the nightstand.

"Yeah," my voice sounded strained to my own ears.

"Damn, Jag, rough night?" Crusher's voice boomed through the phone.

"Fuck you, Crusher, and I say it with nothing but respect for my Prez," I said as I sat up on the side of the bed and ran a hand over my face.

"Sure, it is. And I'll pass on that offer because, brother, you are not my type," Crusher chuckled when I growled into the phone. "Man, I hope whatever has you in a mood works its way out because your ass has to be puckered."

"Don't you have a woman to harass instead of me?" River curled around me and ran her hand up my back. I reached back and placed my hand on her butt and started caressing.

"Hmm, Dom," she moaned, then rubbed against me like a cat.

"Well... well... well. Seems I interrupted something this morning," Crusher said, then added. "Can I say about damn time, Jag?"

"Did your ass call for a reason?"

"River's right, brother. You are an asshole." Crusher chuckled. "But yeah, got a call from Davis. He and his buddies are about two hours out."

"I thought they were due tomorrow."

"They were supposed to be, but they're excited to get here and left sometime yesterday and were going to take their time. Instead, they ended up sharing the driving to get here earlier. A couple of their wives are traveling with them to drive the SUV back while the men ride the bikes. I hope none of them wipe out before they get back home."

"No shit," I said as River's hand slid around and came into contact with my morning wood. Between clenched teeth, I got out, "Well, I'll meet you at the garage in a few." I disconnected the call without giving Crusher a chance to respond.

River moved over, and I laid back down on the bed and pulled her on top of me.

"Do you have to leave?" she asked sleepily.

"Not right away," I said and ran my hands up and down her back.

"Hmm... you promised to show other things."

"That I did, but we crashed before I had the chance. Why don't I take care of that now?" I reached for a condom, put it on in record time, then grabbed hold of her butt and shifted her until my hardness was between her legs.

"Why don't you?"

Feeling relaxed and content for the first time in quite a while. I smiled, rolled us to be on top, then pushed inside her, making good on my promise.

Chapter Twelve

River

After I closed the door, I heard Dom ride off, and I walked toward the kitchen. It was going to take plenty of coffee to deal with the phone call that needed to be made.

With one cup consumed and the cup refilled, I sat on the same stool as last night and picked up my cell.

"Hey, honey. What are you up to?"

"Drinking coffee and talking to you," I said, and my dad chuckled. I took in the sound because when I got done talking, he wouldn't be in the best of moods. But the one thing I could always count on with my dad was support. Any anger he showed would be on my behalf.

"Well, isn't it a coincidence that I am drinking coffee and talking to you," he said, and it was my turn to chuckle.

"Dad, the reason I'm calling is I've got a few things to discuss with you."

"What is going on, River? Has something happened?" The instant concern in his voice was blatant.

"Mother called yesterday evening," I started from the beginning, and my dad listened without too much commentary. Other than the occasional curse word delivered at different times.

When I finished, he was quiet for a few moments, and I knew he was digesting everything I said.

"I'll get the restraining order ready for you to sign. That needs to be filed pronto. I'll go with you on Monday to get it filed. Helps to know the judges in the District Court. As for your mother, honey. She changed after she left here and I'm sorry for her putting you through that. But River..."

"Yeah, Dad?"

"I'm proud of you. You should have called me last night. I would have come over. You shouldn't have been alone, honey."

"I... umm... wasn't," I said tentatively. I'd left that tidbit out initially because I wasn't sure how he would react.

After a brief pause, he said, "I'm going to ask you something, either yes or no will do. I don't want to know more. Were you at Dom's?"

"Yes."

"Okay, I'm glad you weren't alone. And if it matters to you, I like Dom. But even with that, I'm a dad. When I look at you, I see my little girl."

I chuckled. "I love you, Dad."

"Love you too, honey. Hope you have a better day. I got to get ready for work, but if you need me, call."

"I will. Stay safe, Dad."

"Always," he said and hung up.

I took a shower and put on clean clothes, then straightened up my house. Grabbing the bags from shopping the day before, I hung up the few pieces of clothing I purchased, then sat down in the living with bags full of supplies I picked up at the craft store. I couldn't wait to decorate my classroom with some things I had bought.

Just as I finished separating the items and placing the bags beside the desk I had purchased when I first moved in, there was a knock on my door. When I opened the door, Sami stood on the stoop smiling.

"Hi, Sami. Come in." I stepped back, then closed the door after she entered. "What brings you to town?" I asked and led her into the living room to sit down.

"I came by to check on you," Sami said.

"Why?" I asked and frowned.

"Because Dom is going to be busy for a few hours, and he was worried about you. He thought maybe you needed someone to talk to."

"So, he heard? I wondered if he had, but he didn't say anything."

"Only thing he said to me was you had a very upsetting phone call with your mother yesterday," Sami said and shrugged. "I'm sorry if you feel we are overstepping. But, River, you must know how he feels about you. Not to mention I think of you as a friend and I hope you think of me as yours, too," Sami said.

I leaned my head back on the couch and closed my eyes. Dom hadn't shared whatever he heard. He left it up to me if I wanted to mention it. He didn't push for information; he just supported and took care of me. I remember how well he did, too. Time with Dom made everything else insignificant. How couldn't I not know how he felt? It was in every gesture, touch, the way he spoke to me.

"Guess you pulled the short straw?" I opened my eyes, lifted my head, and looked at Sami.

"No. The others don't know. Jag stopped by the house on his way to the shop. Bailey is at work, and Carly started back early this morning. She's covering for one of the other deputies whose wife went into labor. And Luna is at the garage in town updating the books. When I got done doing the few things around the house, I headed to town."

"You didn't have to. But thank you."

"Hey, if you can't unload on your friends, who can you unload on?" Sami said with a smile.

"True. But I really am okay. I don't think I was upset as much as disappointed in my mother. She's difficult on a good day," I started, then shared what the phone call had been about. Sami mainly listened, but like my dad, she dropped the occasional curse word when applicable. While I talked, I alternated between glancing at Sami or staring down at my hands. As I finished telling the last, I felt even better than I had when I dumped on my dad.

"I'm sorry, River, for everything you've been through, but it had to be a load off your chest to say all that to your mother. Give it time. Maybe you and she can work through your issues."

"I doubt it. She won't change, and I'm not going back to the person who always gives in to keep the balance."

"And your ex, I don't think 'sorry' covers his actions. But I am sorry that's the way you found out you couldn't get pregnant."

"Guess I should look on the bright side. I didn't have to go through testing to see why I couldn't. They were going to start with Thomas's sperm count first, then move on to testing me, but his infidelity saved thousands of dollars in doctor bills."

"River..." Sami got up and hugged me. I hugged her back, but knew I needed to get off that subject. Not because it hurt. I figured I'd get a twinge of pain in my heart for a while when reminded that I'd never hold a child of my own.

"I've accepted it, mostly. Sometimes it hits me. But you know what? After you spend month after month doing everything possible to give yourself a better chance to conceive, only to be disappointed each time—it's almost a relief."

"I am glad you are getting a restraining order on your ex. And I would send it to his work, anyway. Fuck him. He should count himself lucky that a little embarrassment is the only thing he has to face," Sami said angrily on my behalf. Which was the difference between friends who stood by you, versus the ones who couldn't get away fast enough when something happens.

"I need to tell Dom before he invests any more time with me." Sami frowned at me, and I rushed on, "Not that I think we are headed down the aisle or even at any stage to talk about kids. I don't want either of us to be hurt if we ever get to that stage," I explained, and Sami still frowned. "What?"

"You can't think that your ability to have children would matter more to Jag than you?"

"How would I know? I'm just getting to know him."

Sami shifted on the couch, bending one of her legs in front of her, allowing her to face me. "I'm going to let you in on a few things. And no, I'm not telling you to keep anything from Jag because I know that information isn't going to make any difference to how he feels. The man really has been out of sorts for a while. We didn't know why at first. I'm talking about us women. The guys more than likely knew, but they are tight-lipped when it comes to each other. Only reason we knew it had to do with a woman is that we caught bits and pieces from walking into rooms while they were giving him shit about his behavior. Luna is the one who figured it out when she witnessed you and Jag together that day in front of Yoga Sensual. She's the one who told us. It answered why he was acting like a butthead. But none of us knew you were Sheriff Lance's daughter. Carly didn't even know. She'd been out recuperating and hasn't been around the station. And she said your dad didn't have any pictures on his desk of you before she went out on leave.

"You need to understand that since I've gotten to know these men, even with women bidding for their attention, they don't let it bother them. Out of the six of them, Jag is the most laid back, easiest to talk to, and hardly ever gets mad. At least until he met you. And, River, these men go after what they want. I experienced it with Kane and watched it happen with the others. Well, except Luna, but it went pretty much the same way since Ghost left with the guys and he came back with her," Sami finished, then shrugged as if adding a 'there you go' to her shared insight on Dom and the others.

"Thanks, Sami, for listening and sharing things about Dom with me."

"Hey, we women have to stick together."

"Yes, we do. After dealing with my mother and reliving some of my rough moments, I deserve a little shopping therapy. If you don't need to get home, we could grab lunch while we're out?"

"Sounds good. No rush for me to get home. I just need to let Kane know. He has Ally. Where do you want to go shopping?" Sami asked.

"I'm thinking I want to get rid of the last thing I have from moving. My car," I said, and Sami's eyebrows shot up.

"Seriously, you want to car shop?"

"Sure do. Clean slate," I said and stood.

"Okay, let's go see if we can get you a good deal," Sami said and stood, too.

It didn't take long to grab the title to my car, then we were out the door and backing out of the driveway.

"Food or hitting the car dealerships first?" I asked and glanced at Sami when she laughed.

"Like you need to ask," Sami said and rubbed her baby bump or the basketball she looked like she was smuggling. "We can eat at Wendy's since it is close to all the dealerships."

"Wendy's it is." I turned on main street and headed in that direction. "Well, at least you're the only one who knows I spent the night at Dom's." When Sami didn't say anything, I glanced over at her, then back to watching the road. "Sami?"

"That I'm not so sure of. I haven't spoken to the others. But Kane was still in the house when Jag stopped by to ask if I would check on you."

"So, you and Kane?"

"And Ally."

"Oh. Guess I didn't make the best impression on one of my students." I immediately thought of the little girl and how she seemed not to have a problem sharing any information.

"Okay, don't be upset that I didn't mention Kane and I knew you had spent the night before Jag stopped by. Ally ratted you out. Her room faces the front, and anytime she hears a bike, she looks out the window. It must have been when he was taking you home and she saw Jag and you leaving. She can't keep anything to herself. She blurted out that you and Uncle Jag must have had a sleepover as soon as she hit the kitchen."

"Great." I would have covered my face if I hadn't been driving.

"Really, don't worry. She was more concerned about why none of her uncles ask her to have a sleepover." Sami laughed.

"I don't know if I'm ready to teach that age."

Sami waved her hand. "You'll do fine. By the end of your first year of teaching, you'll be so used to hearing things you could have gone your whole life without knowing. It will no longer shock you."

I laughed. "Yes, that makes me feel better."

Being with Sami was comfortable. We went to Wendy's and sat down with our food. If trading my car was as easy as spending time with Sami, then my day would be a success.

Chapter Thirteen

Jag

"There goes our first custom bikes, brothers," Flirt said and snapped the cashier's check in his hand.

"Yeah, but not our last. We already have a new order. Parts will be in next week, then we can get started," Crusher said. The six of us and Ally stood in front of Speed's house and watched as the buyers rode away, followed by two of their wives in the SUV they arrived in.

"Hundred bucks says one of them lays his bike down on the ride home," Devil commented.

"Not like any of us hasn't done that at least once," Speed said, and I chuckled.

"I can laugh now, but remember when we were learning to ride, and the dads made us practice on those old dirt bikes first?" At their nods, I continued. "We got tired of them making us stop and start over and over and going through the cones they set up, so we started showing off."

"Oh yeah, because we knew everything about riding. What were we, ten?" Coast asked, then chuckled.

"Glad you guys can find humor from that day. I'm the one who had to spend five hours in the ER getting stitched," Devil replied as we headed back to the garage.

"Umm... because all we did was pick up speed while taking the cones until an enormous dust cloud surrounded the dads. *You* were the one who pulled the front of the bike up for a wheelie and flipped it trying to walk it on the back tire," Crusher said, and everyone laughed except for Devil.

"Uncle Devil, will you teach me how to do that?" Ally asked, causing all of us to jerk our heads in her direction.

"No, he will not!" Speed snapped, then softened his voice. "You can get hurt badly doing that, Ally. Devil had to have his arm stitched and his forehead because the handlebars clipped him as the bike flipped over him. It could have easily landed on him."

Ally nodded to her dad. Then, with her hands on her hips and a serious look on her face, she scanned her eyes over each of us. I could clearly picture her as a grown woman.

"How come boys do dumb stuff?" she asked. We looked at each other, then focused on Speed, and silently asked for help. After the day Ally hanged out with us at the garage and we let her help—we learned moms don't find humor in their little girls caked in oil.

"Women around the world ask that daily. I'm not sure there is an answer," Speed said to her, and she nodded as if that statement alone made all the sense.

"Okay. Am I going to stay with Shakes while you go to Church?" she asked.

"Yes. Shakes is at the clubhouse with Neely, and you'll go home with them. Then I'll pick you up when we're done. You and Neely behave for Shakes, okay?" Speed said.

"'K," Ally answered.

I closed one bay door, and Coast closed the other. After Crusher locked the shop, we headed to the clubhouse.

We didn't talk about club business in front of Ally, so the walk to the clubhouse was relatively quiet. And with Ally around, that was rare and didn't last long. She left her dad's side and moved to mine. I pulled on her ponytail, and she giggled.

"Uncle Jag, do you love me?" she asked, and I smiled when I looked down at her.

"You know I love you, Ally. Why are you asking?" I looked at Speed, and he shrugged. And when I glanced at the others, they were frowning with looks of confusion. I couldn't imagine why she would have any doubt about my feelings for her or any of the others' feelings, either.

"Then how come River gets to have a sleepover and not me?"

Out of the mouth of babes came to mind, and when I heard snickers, I knew my brothers weren't going to offer any help. I looked over to Speed for help.

"Welcome to my world, brother," he smirked.

Wasn't the first time I thought I needed new friends.

I bent, grabbed Ally under the arms, and swung her until she sat on my shoulders.

"I've never had you over for a sleepover because I didn't want your other uncles to think you liked me more or for your dad to think you didn't like the awesome motorcycle bed you have," I said and squeezed her knees where I held her in place. When I glanced at the others, I smiled, and they sneered. I would no doubt hear their responses once Ally was out of earshot.

"Oh yeah. Maybe it would be better if all of you came for a sleepover at my house. Can we do that, Daddy?" she asked, and I looked to Speed and mouthed sorry for throwing him under the bus. I shouldn't have worried about my brother; he was used to dealing with his daughter.

"Sure, but you'll have to clear that with your momma," Speed replied as we reached the back door to the clubhouse. From the sound of the bikes in the distance, it sounded like most of the members were going to make the meeting.

I set Ally on her feet, and she ran inside to find Neely as soon as I opened the door.

"Nice save with Ally, but Sami is going to kill you when Ally bugs the shit out of her for a sleepover," Speed said as he walked past. As we made our way inside, he stopped in the kitchen to speak with Shakes. The rest of us continued through the clubhouse to the large room that was located off the main one in the front of the clubhouse.

When we started the construction on the building that held Soft Tails, we decided to turn the bar area into a bar that served food. We also opened it up to the locals. The new Soft Tails strip club would be in the recent addition added to the back. It would have its own public entrance there, and a private one for club members only to use from the bar side.

With the changes, we would now hold Church at the clubhouse. For privacy, we converted the game room into a meeting room. The club was growing. Black Hawk hadn't had a lot of members with ol' ladies when it first started. But as the years passed by, that changed, too.

"Dad said before they bought the building and opened Soft Tails, they held Church here. They moved it to the bar when the club grew, and a lot of the members lived in town. Plus, it was easier for the ones working for the other businesses to attend," Crusher said as we reached the main room and brothers were coming in the door.

"Yeah, my dad said the same thing," I said as I walked through the doorway into the larger room. "Damn, the prospects did a good job of cleaning and setting this place up."

The two pool tables sat to one side in their own area, sticks hung on the wall rack between the tables. The card tables would serve as seating tables when Church was held. I walked to the bar on the back wall and ran my hand over the top.

"Ghost and Dare got it finished. Looks good, doesn't it?" Flirt stated.

"Talk about a business that is going to flourish once the word gets out on what they can do," Devil said as he stepped behind the bar.

Crusher and I walked to the table in the room's front, and Devil and Flirt followed. When Speed walked in, the rest of the members who had just arrived entered behind him. Everyone sat and waited for Crusher to sit and start the meeting.

When the four of us sat, Speed and Coast pulled the doors closed and stood on each side of them. Crusher banged the gavel and Church began.

As I listened, my mind wandered to River. I couldn't wait to see her again. I knew once the meeting was over, I wouldn't hang around to bullshit. There was a better place for me to be.

Crusher informed everyone that Church would now be held on Friday evenings. Partying could start after for the ones who stayed around. He also reminded everyone that there were now small kids that came through, so they needed to be mindful.

"VP is going to fill you in on what's going on with the club businesses," Crusher finished.

"First, I want to acknowledge Ghost and Dare for the fine bar they built. We all know it holds what most of you come to Church for." I waited for everyone to yell out their thanks and cheer over the bar, then continued. "The gym is ready to open as soon as they do the last inspection next week. The massage side is finished and ready to open. It only needs a few masseuses. We've received a lot of resumes and narrowed it down to ten for interviews."

"VP, I volunteer to be the interviewer," Roscoe said, and the entire room chuckled.

"As entertaining as that would be, Roscoe, Ghost's and Speed's ol' ladies will conduct those. They will be more apt in hiring the most qualified, instead of who has the best assets to look at." I laughed at all the groans in the room. "The bar is doing well on its own, but it will do better when the strip club side is done, which is slated in four weeks. Boss and Turk are closing on the building for the cannabis store. If all goes well, it will be up and running in three months. There's only one more thing to mention, but I'm going to let our treasurer inform you because he hasn't released the check in his hand since it was handed to him."

Everyone laughed when Flirt held his hand up, showing the check he still clutched.

"With this check I hold, Sons of Black Hawk Custom Rides is officially in the black. The first bikes rode away from the compound this morning. There are already new orders to take their place. Now I give the floor back to Prez."

"Well, I say we christen the bar," Crusher said and banged the gavel, putting an end to Church.

"I'll be at River's if you guys need me," I said.

"Coast, guess it is you and I left. Another is on his way down," Flirt said, and I flipped him off.

"We wanted to tell you, boys, how proud we are of you," Stroker said as he and the other dads walked up.

After one arm hugs and chatting, I made my break, eager to see River.

"You heading to town to see River?" my dad said as I took my first step toward the door.

"How do you know about River?"

"Let's just say the girl is determined to run over an Amara."

"What?" I asked, and my dad filled me in on his close call. I couldn't help but laugh.

"You should be okay if you stay out of her way while she's driving," he said and chuckled.

"Yeah, I do that. You call if you need me," I told him, and my dad nodded.

"Same goes. And stay out of trouble."

"Depends on what kind you're talking about," I said and smacked his shoulder.

Before anyone else had time to stop me, I went through the front door, then skirted the side of the clubhouse to head to my house. Ten minutes later, I was on my way to River's.

Riding down River's street, I frowned when I saw Sami and River standing by a large, black Cadillac Escalade that was in her driveway parked beside Sami's car. They had the doors open, looking inside it. Both women turned and smiled as I reached the driveway and pulled up behind the SUV.

River was talking before I even got the bike shut off. Once I dismounted, I pulled my helmet off and placed it on the seat.

"Do you like it?" River asked as she waved her hand out like a game show host, making Sami laugh.

"Great, did you get that monster so the next time you try to take out my dad or me, you won't miss?" I grinned when she glared at me.

"That didn't take long to get back to you. Did he tell you it was his and the others' fault because they were crossing in the wrong spot?"

I bit the inside of my cheeks to keep from laughing at her putout look. "Well, at least I won't have to worry about you get hurting in an accident," I said, then as I got closer to her, I placed my hand on her neck and bent down and kissed her.

"Are you insinuating that I can't drive?" she responded when I released her.

"I plead the fifth," I said as I moved to look over the vehicle.

"Spoken like a true attorney," River said and followed me around the SUV.

"No, I spoke it like a man hoping to have more sex soon."

"Dom!" River yelled at me, then turned toward Sami when she laughed.

"I think that is my cue to leave," Sami said.

I opened the driver's side door and sat in the seat, which I had to slide back to fit. "Very nice. I didn't know you wanted to trade vehicles. If you'd told me, I would have gone with you," I said as I looked at the dash. The sucker had every bell and whistle.

"Sami did. I'm going to let it slide that you seem to imply I'm incapable of buying a vehicle without a man."

"Again, I plead the fifth." River made a huffing sound, and my lips twitched.

"Uh... Jag, she got a fantastic deal. I am in awe of her skill." I looked over at Sami, who stood at the opened passenger door.

"Hershel Stevens gives no one a good deal."

"Hershel probably went home and cried after River left," Sami said with a laugh.

"No shit." I looked between the two women.

"I got him to come down on the price of the Escalade, and then I got them to give me top dollar for the Mercedes. It was a straight swap," River said and smiled widely. "No way Mr. Stevens made it home before he cried. He had tears in his eyes when he handed me the keys."

"Well, then let's take this baby for a spin, and celebrate your fantastic deal," I said just as my cell rang. "After I take this call." I slid out of the vehicle.

As I looked down at the screen, I frowned when only an out of state number showed. I swiped the screen and moved down the driveway to have some privacy.

"Amara," I answered.

"Dominic Amara?" the man asked with a shakiness in his voice.

"Yes."

"This is Norman Blankenship."

"Mr. Blankenship, I'm not sure why you're calling?" I asked and looked over my shoulder to see Sami and River opening the back of the vehicle. I wasn't sure why Simone's dad was calling me. I hadn't talked with him since I turned down his job offer. And Simone and I hadn't spoken since she walked out of my townhouse when we ended our relationship.

"Dom, I... I'm not sure what to say. Simone is dead." His voice broke, and I wasn't sure what the man wanted me to say. I felt bad about the news, but...

"Sorry to hear that, Mr. Blankenship, but you must know Simone and I haven't spoken since before I left. So, I'm a little confused on why you felt you needed to contact me."

"No... no. I'm sorry, I'm not explaining this well at all." I heard him take a deep breath.

"Explain what?"

"Goddammit, I told Simone she needed to tell you, but she refused. Dom Poppy is in the hospital. She's in an induced coma, she—"

"Who the fuck is Poppy!?" I asked, cutting him off. The man was making no sense.

"My granddaughter, Dom," he informed me, then added. "Your daughter."

"Say what? My daughter?" My entire world shifted in that moment.

"Yes, your daughter."

I ran a hand over my face. How was it possible? She had my daughter and didn't bother to tell me. Everything went through my head at once. I took a deep breath.

"Tell me everything," I said, calmer than I actually felt.

"Simone was crossing the street with Poppy in her stroller. The crossing light lit up, and they moved off the sidewalk. A taxi was already turning right, and the driver stopped. But a car ran the red light, and they think the taxi blocked Simone from seeing it. The driver of the car slammed on his brakes, but it was too late. Simone took most of the impact. Poppy's stroller was knocked over. She was strapped in, and they said that along with the fact the driver got the car stopped is what saved her from being hurt more. She hit her head on the pavement when the stroller fell over. If the car hadn't stopped, the stroller would have been run over.

"Like I said before, she is in an induced coma because of swelling, and they don't want her to move around while they work to get it to go down."

"What hospital?" He said the name when I asked. "I'll be there as soon as I can get a flight out. I'll expect to have all questions answered when I get there." I didn't wait for him to reply before I disconnected the call.

I squatted down and put my hands on my thighs. Bowing my head, taking deep breaths. *A daughter.*

"Dom, are you okay?" River asked as she touched my shoulder.

I stood, and River's hand dropped from my shoulder to my arm. Sami was off to the side, talking on her phone.

"You heard?"

"Yes, enough to get the gist of what happened."

"Shit!" I yelled and threw my phone. It hit the street and shattered. "I've got a daughter, and I only find out because she is in the fucking hospital in a coma." I rub my face with both hands. "Who the fuck doesn't tell someone they have a kid? I didn't even ask how old she is. I need to go to her, but I'm not sure what to do first."

River wrapped her arms around me, and I latched on to her. She rubbed my back with one hand and ran her other hand over my head that I laid on her shoulder.

"Take a minute and just breathe. That's all you've got to do right this second. When you're ready, I'll help in any way you need."

Did she even know how her words affected me? There was no way I could find the words right then to tell her. What would I have done if she hadn't been here? I was supposed to be the one helping her.

"I've got to go to her. I'm going to take the first flight I can get on," I said as I raised my head and looked at River.

"I can search for flights online while you go home and pack a bag. You broke your cell. You can take mine, and if you tell me your cell plan info, I'll get it replaced while you're gone. Do you want me to drive you to the airport?"

"Jag? Speed, Coast, and your dad are here," Sami said. And by the time what she said registered, my dad's truck pulled up. At least that answered who she'd been talking with on the phone.

Speed and Coast both gave me the typical man hug when they reached me. Not my dad. He grabbed and pulled me into his arms.

"You got this, son. I'll be with you every step of the way," he said against my ear.

When we broke apart, I shared everything I knew.

"Damn, Jag. Whatever you need, brother. You shouldn't be riding. I'll ride your bike back," Coast said. I wanted to argue I was fine to ride my damn bike, but I wasn't. I was functioning on autopilot. Reaching inside my pocket, I handed over my key.

"Jag, take however much time you need to take care of your daughter. Don't worry about the club or anything else right now. We got your back, brother," Speed said, and I nodded.

"You ready to go, son? We need to pack a bag and get to the airport," my dad said. He was correct. I turned and saw River standing off to the side with Sami. I hadn't realized she'd moved away when the others arrived.

I walked over to her, leaned down, and kissed her. "Thank you. Not sure I'd be able to think if you hadn't been here."

"Yes, you would have."

"I have to go."

"I know you do," she said and gave me a half smile.

"Come with me," was out of my mouth as soon as I thought about it. River affected me like no other woman had. And the thought of going anywhere without her put knots in my stomach. While I waited for her to answer, the one part of me that hoped she'd refuse to go fought with the other part that wanted her there.

"Dom, you don't need me there. Your focus needs to be on Poppy." River touched my arm and rubbed.

"I don't know anything about taking care of a baby. What am I supposed to do?" I asked and moved her hand off my arm, only to grab both her hands with mine.

"You're just overwhelmed. Once you get there and see her, everything will fall into place."

I knew it wasn't rational to put River on the spot, but at the moment, she felt like a lifeline to me. And if she weren't by my side, I would drown.

"Please come with me. I want you there. I need you there," I said, and River looked at Sami who only shrugged.

I glanced over my shoulder at Speed, Coast, and my dad.

"Say yes, girl, so we can get it in gear," my dad said, and I turned back to River.

"You all realize this is crazy, right? I've known him for a total of three days. And I'm supposed to get on a plane and travel across the country to meet his daughter, whom he didn't know about."

"Does your babbling mean you are considering it?" I asked, and River stared at me.

"I might be able to sway her," my dad said, then looked at River. "That your new vehicle beside Sami's car?" he asked her, and I frowned.

"Yes." I noticed River was frowning, too.

"Nice. Will you make my boy happy if I stand in the road and let you back into me?" River didn't answer. She just stared at my dad.

"Dad, enough," I said, but kept my eyes on River. "Sorry, he's just trying to lighten the mood."

River looked back at me. "Good, we're going to need his humor for the long ass flight." It was my turn to stare.

"That a girl! Live in the moment," my dad said, then cupped her face and kissed her forehead. "Thanks, darlin'. I think he does need you."

I still held River's hands, and I gave them a squeeze, drawing her attention back to me as my dad stepped away.

"You're really coming?"

"Yes, which if we don't get a move on it, I may change my mind. You go with your dad and get want you're taking. I need to pack a bag and call my dad and tell him I'll be out of town. Neither one of you needs to drive, so we will take my vehicle to the airport. I'll need it there anyway, because I'm not sure how long I'll get to stay. I've got to get things ready before schools starts."

"You're amazing," I said and kissed her cheek. "See you, in, say, an hour?"

"That should work," River answered.

"While we're waiting on you, I'll go online and book the tickets," my dad said, then started toward his truck.

"Thank you," I said, kissed her once again, then turned to the others. "Ready to go?"

"Coast will follow you and your dad. Sami and I will wait on River, and she can follow us to the compound," Speed said.

"Thanks, brother. I didn't even think of that."

"You got other things much more pressing on your mind. Now get going, you have a daughter to meet," Speed said, slapped me on the back and followed River and Sami into the house.

I walked to my dad's truck as Coast started up my bike. My dad pulled out once I was in the truck and Coast pulled out behind us.

In a few hours, I would be on my way to meet my daughter. It seemed surreal.

Chapter Fourteen

River

Dom and his dad were ready and waiting as I pulled up to Dom's house. I was glad Speed and Sami stayed while I put together a bag, because I would have missed the turnoff otherwise.

The drive to the airport was a somber one with benign conversation to pass the time. As I drove, it gave me a chance to observe the relationship between Dom and Flyboy. What I witnessed was a father and son with similar personalities. As they spoke, there was also no doubt of their love or support for each other. It didn't escape me that my dad and I shared the same. The only difference was Flyboy raised Dom while my dad had to parent at a distance.

I called my dad to let him know I would be out of town. If he was shocked about me going, it didn't show. He just gave his support as usual, told me he was there if I needed him, and to tell Dom the same. I'd forgotten about filing the restraining order until he mentioned it. And I promised it would be the first thing I took care of when I returned. I also left a message with the principal of the school, saying I had to go out of town for an emergency but would be back in plenty of time before school started.

When we reached the airport and checked in, our wait to board wasn't long. Flyboy had gotten us on a straight flight that left no time for any delay in getting to the airport. Which worked, but only first-class seats were available on the flight. I sat with Dom, and his dad sat in the seat across the aisle.

The flight was long, but the time passed as we discussed the plan for once we were on the ground. Flyboy had reserved a rental car when he made the flight arrangements. I used on flight internet to secure two rooms in a hotel down the street from the hospital. Depending on what was going on with Poppy when we got there, we would need a place for our bags and to catch some sleep.

Throughout the flight, Dom was subdued. Other than participating in the plan of action, he stayed in his own thoughts. I couldn't blame him with his situation. It was a lot to take in, and he would need to be prepared for what lay ahead.

I was mentally exhausted, and I knew Dom had to be, too.

Once we landed, we walked past baggage claim and headed straight for airport transit and jumped on the bus that would drop us off at the rental car place. Flyboy took care of the paperwork, and with directions to where the rental was located, we headed out of the building.

As we drove to the hotel, no one spoke, the trip taking its toll on the three of us. And it was only the start.

Checked into the hotel, we rode the elevated to our floor. Finding the room numbers, which luckily for us were beside each other, I stepped in front of the door to my room. As I swiped my key card and pushed the door the open, Dom and his dad did the same to the door next to mine.

In my room, I set my bag on the end of one bed, then grabbed what I needed out of it to freshen up. A shower would have to wait. There was no time. Dom needed to get to the hospital.

I started toward the bathroom, and a knock on my door stopped me. When I reached the door and opened it, Dom stepped forward, and I made room for him to enter. That's when I noticed he held his bag.

"Dom, why do you have your bag?" I asked. My face had to hold the look of confusion since I'd seen him go into the other room.

"I want to stay here. With you," he said and set his bag on the spare bed. Then he sat on the edge of the other bed and rested his arms across his lap.

"Dom, your dad. He—"

"Can sleep alone," he finished my sentence.

"You got a lot on your mind, Dom. Not sure us sharing a room is the answer," I said, as I stood by the bathroom door. With the look on his face and the slump of his shoulders, all I wanted to do was wrap my arms around him and tell him it would work out.

"Yeah, and the next little bit is going to add to it. So, I need to be with you to balance it out. River, I know you're confused about why I wanted you here. I'm confused, too. Do you think I don't know it is moving fast between us? Christ, a couple of run-ins, and a couple days together doesn't mean we know each other. So the fact that I feel I need to have you near makes no sense. I follow a set of rules as a lawyer. As the VP of the club, I follow a set of rules. As a man, I follow my set of rules. But with each, you also must follow your instincts. And my instincts lead to you."

"I bet when you walk into a courtroom, the opposing attorney cringes." My words received a half smile. "We probably won't spend a lot of time here, anyway. So, okay."

"It doesn't matter. When we are here, I want to be with you."

The way he said it was simple, but my mind said it was anything but. When less than six months ago, my world crumbled, two months ago I literally ran into the man, and in three days—with him in front of me—I felt content. How can anyone trust that?

"I want to get to the hospital as soon as we freshen up," he stood and moved to his bag and unzipped it.

"I won't be long," I said, then walked into the bathroom, tired, confused, and no closer to an answer to my feelings for Dom.

Jag

The hospital doors opened with a swish, and I walked through. On our way to the hospital, Mr. Blankenship called to let me know he had approved my visitation, and a badge would be ready at the waiting desk for the PICU (Pediatric Intensive Care Unit). It drove home that I had a daughter with no legal claim to her.

That would be rectified soon enough.

I informed Simone's dad there would be two others that needed to be added to Poppy's visitation. After I gave him my dad's and River's names and received his word that it would be taken care of it, I disconnected the call.

We made our way to the floor where the PICU was located. Once we had our badges, a nurse led us to where Poppy was. When we walked in, Mr. Blankenship sat in a chair by the crib-shaped bed that held a small form.

"There was no change through the night. No worse, no better. They say that is good, means the meds in her IV are working."

I heard my dad's voice as he talked with Mr. Blankenship, but I didn't care what was being said. My attention was on my daughter, Poppy. Her head had a small bandage wrapped around it, leaving the top uncovered.

Short, dark brown curls could be seen. Her skin was golden like mine. With her eyelids shut, I did not know what the color of her eyes were.

In her facial features, I saw parts of Simone and me combined. God, I wanted to lift her and hold her tight and take away every hurt she had.

"She is beautiful, Dom," River said as she moved beside me, placing a hand on my arm.

I couldn't speak, so I nodded. I touched the one arm that wasn't bandaged, careful not to hit the tube taped to her skin.

"Dom?" At my dad saying my name, I looked up at him, but his eyes were on Poppy. I felt my emotions, but my dad's showed on his face, telling me he felt as I did.

"I know," I whispered, then gathered my thoughts and turned to Mr. Blankenship.

"I'm sorry, Dom. This isn't the way a man should meet his daughter for the first time. I know you are angry, and I will answer any questions you have."

"Damn straight you will," I snapped, and River squeezed my arm.

"Don't let Poppy's first time hearing your voice be because you are angry."

"Yeah." I leaned over and kissed the top of River's head, and I caught the question in Simone's dad's eyes. "River is my ol' lady," I answered his silent question.

I could feel River's eyes on me, and when I looked, her brows were furrowed.

"Don't panic, it is the easiest explanation," I said in a low voice by her ear.

"River," Mr. Blankenship said and nodded his head to acknowledge her.

"Mr. Blankenship."

"Please, call me Norman. We're going to be spending a good amount of time with each other for the foreseeable future."

A nurse stepped in and informed us we would have to step out for the upcoming shift change. We could return in an hour and a half.

"We could go to the cafeteria," River brought up, and I nodded along with my dad.

"If you don't mind, I'll join you. I could use some coffee. Plus, it will give us a chance to talk," Norman said.

"Yes, we need to talk," I said, reaching for River's hand and linked our fingers. Once the badges were turned in, the four of us headed to the cafeteria. As we walked, Norman told us about Poppy's birth, to include the date, the time, and her weight. My suspicion was right, at barely eleven months for Poppy's age, Simone was three months pregnant when I left. She'd known before I left and couldn't be bothered to let me know.

The four of us sat at a table as off the grid as possible to have some privacy.

"I've had plenty of time to think before arriving here, Norman. I didn't head home until two months after Simone and I ended our relationship. She knew she carried my child while I was still here."

"Yes."

"I am sorry for your loss, Norman. I know you are burying your daughter, but goddamn, my daughter could have died, and I wouldn't have known about her. Simone had her flaws, but I wouldn't have believed her capable of this. And you, why didn't you inform me? I not only had a fucking right to know, I had a right to decide on how I would be in Poppy's life. Both were fucking taken from me. And I wasn't the only one shorted. My dad missed... what, a year, with his granddaughter? I didn't even know her age or the date she was born until now. I know nothing that deals with her because others made that fucking choice!"

"Dom," River said.

"What?" I turned to her and snapped. River's eyes went wide, and I felt like shit. "I'm sorry, River."

"I know it's because you are angry but, Dom, you're here now with Poppy. I'm not dismissing that the whole situation is shitty. You can't make up the time no matter how mad you get. People do crappy things to other people. And though Norman was involved, and you want to lash out at him for that, it's nothing compared to the punishment of having to bury his daughter," River paused and looked at Norman, "because no parent should have to bury their child. And yes, Poppy could have died, but she didn't. You can't dwell on what could have happened."

I looked at Norman and knew River was right. The man had dark circles under his eyes. He looked worn out and dealing with Simone's death, and Poppy in the hospital, had taken its toll on him.

"Want I'm trying to say, is that things happen that are out of our control. But once given the opportunity, we decide how it gets handled from that point," River said, then picked up her coffee cup and took a drink.

"River's right, son. You can only go forward," my dad said and patted River's arm that rested on the table.

"Yeah, she is. Glad she came with us. She might be the only one to keep us out of trouble."

"No, even I'm not that good," she said behind the coffee cup she'd lifted to her mouth.

I chuckled, my dad laughed, and Norman snorted. Even in serious situations, sometimes you needed to take a moment to just be.

"Since we have twenty minutes left before we can go upstairs, I'd like to get through everything, so we can spend our time seeing to Poppy. First, she will go home with me. I won't keep you from seeing her, but you will need to come to Shades Valley. Second, when the doctor makes his rounds, I'm going to have them take a swab from Poppy and me. Going to need the DNA to get my name added to her birth certificate since Simone is deceased. I still have some contacts around here, so I should be able to expedite anything I need to be done. I'd like to get any running I have to do before they wake Poppy. Because I will not want to leave her if I don't have to. That's where I stand on things, Norman." I laid everything on the table. I needed to know if I was going to have to fight Norman.

"I will not fight you on taking Poppy. She needs to be with a parent. I'm her grandad and I love that little girl, but I know my limits. I still had some youth when Simone's mother died, and I had to raise her by myself. I don't have that energy now. I'm a workaholic, which would put Poppy being raised by a nanny more than by me. With her across the country, it might be good for me. It will force me to take a vacation now and then, so I can visit her. If your contacts can't help you get things done before Poppy is ready to travel, let me know. Got a few contacts that owe me favors," Norman finished speaking and looked at his watch, then continued. "It's about time to go back up, but I need to go by the funeral home to deal with Simone's burial. I'll try to get back before the doctor makes rounds. When I come back though, I'll bring all the documents you're going to need for Poppy. Also, I imagine you'll be flying home, so later we can talk about when you want to get Poppy's things boxed and sent to your house." Norman stood, and I checked the clock on the cafeteria's wall and did the same.

"Don't rush to get back, Norman. I'll let you know what the doctor says if you miss him."

Norman shook hands with me, then my dad, and left to take care of his business. Dad stood and stretched as I held the chair for River. The three of us rode the elevator up and then stopped by the desk for the badges we needed.

No doubt the entire process would become a routine before they released Poppy.

Chapter Fifteen

Jag

"Is she waking?" River asked as she rushed into the room.

"No. You're flushed. Did you run here?" I asked from the chair beside Poppy's bed.

"Damn near. We picked up the badges and before I even got mine on, she was gone. I tried to catch up, but the girl is fast," my dad said when he walked in, clipping the badge to his t-shirt.

"Hey, it's not my fault you're out of shape," River said, and I chuckled when my dad raised a brow and glared at her.

Each day that passed by while we'd been there, I watched River and my dad grow closer. At first, I admit, it made me a tad jealous that she seemed to grow closer to him than me. But it didn't take long for me to realize she goaded him to get him focused on something else when the stress seemed to get the best of him.

That's when I noticed she did the same with me, but instead of goading me, she touched me. It was anything from resting her hand on my arm to moving the hair off my forehead, or she'd place her hand on my back and rub over the muscles that would tense while I watched the medical team wheel Poppy away for tests. I learned a long time ago it was the small things that, when added together, made the biggest impact.

"I told you on the phone that it wouldn't happen right away. They stopped the meds keeping her under along with all the other stuff hooked up to her. Except for the monitor. Besides, the doctor said it was better for her to come around on her own than for them to force it," I said and smiled as I watched her run her fingers over the tiny curls on top of my daughter's head. I wondered briefly if Poppy felt as soothed as I did when River touched me.

"Oh my God, Dom, I think I saw her eyes twitching behind her eyelids," River said while continuing to touch Poppy's hair. "Come on, sweet girl. Don't you want to meet your daddy and grandpa?"

River had no clue about the effect she had on others. Or it was possible the effect she had on Amara men. I glanced across the bed at my dad and knew I wore the same expression his face did to River's words.

"Did you get ahold of Norman?" my dad asked.

"Yes, he said he would be here as soon as the graveside service was over for Simone."

One week had passed. Every day was monotonous. I spent every spare second I had at Poppy's side. When I wasn't with Poppy, it was to either run to the hotel to shower or to get the things ready for when I'd get to take her home.

There were times I wanted to punch something, like when they came in and changed Poppy's bandages. It was hard to watch, but for her, I'd do it. The first time her head was revealed, I'd gotten my first look at the stitches and the bald spot where her head had been shaved about brought me to my knees. They removed the one on her arm and the sight of the skin bruised, and sporting road rash down the length of her arm, had my hands clenching into fists. I only relaxed after the doctor said her head and arm were healing nicely.

Simone's penance for high-end items paid off in the stroller she'd bought. The padding on the head guard kept Poppy's head injury from being so much worse. Just as the padding on the sides saved her arm from being broken. She'd only received the road rash on her arm because it fell out before the stroller had stopped skidding.

I was over questioning. At that point, I was glad she survived, and nothing else mattered.

One bright spot of the week was the photo album Norman brought in for me. It was filled with pictures of Poppy from birth to a few more current ones from last month.

Norman had other news that day, too. They charged the bastard who ran the red light with vehicular manslaughter. He'd spend one year, possibly three, in jail. He told the cops at the scene that the light had just turned yellow as he was going through it. The tape at the intersection showed him on his cell phone and the light turning red before he reached it.

A little jail time was better than nothing, I was told. To me, he deserved the death penalty. Norman had already started the paperwork to file a civil suit. Anything granted would go placed in a trust account for Poppy.

Five hours had gone by since River noticed the first twitch from Poppy. With only three other instances occurring, it made the wait seem forever.

"I'm glad I didn't miss her waking up and sad at the same time that she wasn't awake when I walked in," Norman said as he stepped closer to the bed. "When you called this morning and informed me they were taking her off the drugs to let her wake, a little part of me thought it was a sign. How stupid am I to have thought Poppy would wake while I was saying goodbye to her mom today?"

River turned her face into my chest, and I rubbed her back while she cried at Norman's words. I placed a hand on the man's shoulder and squeezed. Whatever anger I felt toward Norman for any part he played in Simone's deception left me.

"Hey, look!" At the anxiousness in my dad's voice, I glanced at him. His eyes were focused on Poppy.

River turned in my arms and the four of us watched as Poppy's eyes blinked.

"Talk to her, Dom," River said and elbowed me.

"I don't want to scare her and make her cry. The nurse told me not to get my feelings hurt if she cried."

"If she does, then talk to her until she calms."

I took a deep breath, blew it out, then leaned forward, so Poppy could see my face when her eyes opened.

"Hi, baby girl. You're doing good. Open your beautiful brown eyes I've only seen in pictures."

"Come on, Poppy. If you open your eyes, I'll buy you a motorcycle as soon as you're able to ride," my dad said.

"And I'll buy you a pony, Pop," Norman said.

"Seriously, a pony?" I snorted.

"Hey, she'll be living with you. So why not?" Norman chuckled, as did River.

"Poppy, you need to wake up, sweet girl. Bet you could get these three men to promise you enough animals for your own zoo if you show them your eyes."

"You're not helping," I said and shook my head. What did I know about eleven-month-old babies? But I hoped Poppy wouldn't understand what her grandpas were saying.

We kept talking to Poppy, and before long, her legs moved, then her arms. All the while her eyes sporadically opened and closed until finally, with a few seconds of continuous blinking, her eyes popped open. I would never forget the moment I saw my daughter's eyes for the first time.

The four of us stopped talking and watched Poppy move those eyes to each of us. Then her mouth opened, and she wailed. No lead up warning like a whine or a little fussing. Nope, it was a full on cry.

"Shush, you're alright," River cooed and ran her hand over Poppy's hair. It didn't escape me that the three of us men froze with Poppy's cries. I also realized it didn't matter what age a female was, I didn't like tears. Poppy's went way past not liking. Her tears gutted me. As a man, I felt useless.

The nurse came in and looked at the monitor, then checked Poppy. Before she left, she told us the doctor would be in shortly to check her over.

The end of week one came to a close.

Week two at the hospital started, and it was a lot of things, but dull wasn't one of them.

There were highs and lows. I enjoyed the highs; the lows sucked ass. Being able to hold Poppy, hear her laugh, see her smile, read her a book, and her playing with her favorite toys that Grandpa Norman had brought from the house, even her blowing spit bubbles, were all highs. Poppy crying and her arms reaching out as they took her to run a scan on her head, her barfing on me, and her poop running down my shirt because I didn't get the diaper on tight enough, were all lows. But Poppy bawling, and none of us being able to console her because she missed her mom— nothing was worse than that. At least I thought so until...

"Dom, I'm going home at the end of the week. The superintendent emailed me and there are three workshops the board wants me to attend next week. I can't miss them," River said when I walked out of the bathroom of the hotel room.

We'd left the hospital while the PICU went through shift change and left my dad there. It was his turn to stay close by. The four of us had been rotating turns.

"Time is going to drag by."

"No, it won't. Poppy will keep you busy. She's getting more active every day. She only has a small bandage on her head, and its purpose is more so she doesn't accidentally scratch the area before they remove the stitches out. The doctor said the swelling is gone, and she shows no signs the head injury caused any motor skill damage. Even the road rash is almost healed. The only thing noticeable are the bruises, and it is because they are multicolored, but they're healing, too."

"I know all that. I meant without you." I looked around the room. "You were right about the hotel room. Other than using it to shower and store our clothes, we didn't get to use it much. Except for the two quickies, which were worth every dollar spent for the room. I'm going to miss the quickies," I said as I pulled my jeans up.

"I think you can survive a week," she said and rolled her eyes.

"I know that here," I pointed to my head when River looked at me, then pointed to the front of my jeans, "but not here." I laughed when the towel hit me, she'd had wrapped around her head.

Two days later, River flew home. And week two officially ended.

She said I'd survive week three without her. I wasn't so sure I could.

Chapter Sixteen

Jag

Week three at the hospital started out slow. By the middle of the week, we were scrambling when we got the go for Poppy to fly. I bought tickets immediately. Norman had packed a bag for Poppy last week when he had her other things packed and shipped to my house. All of it was due to arrive the day before we got back.

When I called to give an update to Crusher, he told me not to worry, they would get Poppy's room put together.

Poppy's release date arrived, and I'd never been so happy to leave a place or so exhausted.

At the airport, Norman said goodbye to Poppy. I'm not sure in his shoes I would have done the same.

Seated in first class, with my seat leaned back, my daughter dozing, I closed my eyes. I could feel the last of my body's energy draining.

"I like River. She's good with Poppy, too. But most of all, I'm not sure you and I would have gotten by the first week without her," my dad said and leaned his seat back.

"I like her, too, Dad," I answered without opening my eyes.

"Are you going to do something about that?" he asked.

"Working on it."

"Need me to put in a good word for you?"

I cracked an eye open and looked at my dad. "Nah, I'm good."

"I'm always here for you, Dom."

"I know, Dad. And if I haven't mentioned it, thanks for making the trip with me."

"No place else I would have been."

"I will be glad to get Poppy home. Her room is ready. Crusher called and told this morning and to check if we were going to need a ride to the compound."

"It will be good for Poppy to have familiar things around. It'll make it easier for her to settle in."

"I hope so. That's why River's picking us. I called to let her know we were heading home. She mentioned it might be good if Poppy sees a familiar face when we land. Plus, she misses her."

"You're not doing something right if Poppy is the only one she misses," my dad said and chuckled.

"She cares. I see it in her eyes. But her saying it may take a while."

"River may surprise you, Dom. I taught you to never underestimate a woman."

"I'm not sure I can take any more surprises."

River

As Dom drove, he kept glancing in the rearview mirror at me. The desire I saw was for me, but I wasn't sure after I told him of the week I had after I'd gotten back, it would still be there. And it scared me more than I wanted to think about.

I'd picked them up at the airport, nervous about seeing him, yet curious at the same time. I needed to know if the feelings that grew while we'd been together, taking care of Poppy, were because of the circumstance or because of him.

From the way he hugged and kissed me at the airport, it was him. But as I sat in the back seat with Poppy, keeping her entertained, doubt pushed through. Brought on from the little left of my old self. Even knowing didn't help me push it back.

Regardless of the swirling feelings I was dealing with, I wouldn't put off telling him. Not after what he just went through, and playing games wasn't who I was, anyway.

The truck slowed, then turned, and I didn't need to look to know my time for musing was about to end. We'd arrived at Black Hawk.

We dropped Flyboy off at his place, then pulled up in front of Dom's house. I carried Poppy in, who had fallen asleep, and Dom grabbed his and Poppy's bags.

The air between us felt chilled, and I knew Dom was feeling it too, because neither one of us had spoken on the way to his house from Flyboy's.

"What going on, River?" Dom asked as soon as he closed the front door.

I looked down at Poppy, then back at him. "I need to talk with you. But it can wait until Poppy is settled."

"Just say what you have to say. Then you can go. I have Poppy now. And I'm too tired for anything else," he said, then took Poppy from my arms.

"I know you have her. I was there, remember?"

He didn't answer. Instead, he headed for the stairs, and I followed.

"Let me help you put her down?"

"Fine." The clipped answer was a sign he was running out of patience.

I followed him into the room that was now Poppy's. I don't know what I expected, but a completely set up room as though she always lived there was a surprise.

"Who did this?" I asked as Dom laid Poppy gently down in her crib. She didn't even move. I grabbed a diaper while Dom opened drawers until he found her pajamas.

"The guys and the women," he answered as we worked together, getting Poppy ready for bed. Through the entire process, Poppy slept.

"I can't believe she didn't wake up," I commented as we left the room.

"She had a busy day. She's exhausted. So am I, so let's get this over with," he said, then headed down the stairs. I followed him downstairs and into the living room.

This was not that man who kissed me at the airport as if he needed me to breathe. Not even the same man who looked at me in the rearview mirror with eyes full of desire.

I sat on one corner of the couch, and he took the other. When I didn't immediately speak, he raised a brow.

I wiped my hands on my pants, then clasped them on my lap. I could do this, was what I thought. The woman who did what everyone else expected her to was no longer me.

"I'm not sure how much of the phone call with my mother you overheard? We never discussed it."

"Enough to know your ex cheated and blamed you," he said, and I nodded.

"Yes, he did. He also got the woman pregnant."

"Jesus. River, the situation with Simone and Poppy, you—"

"No! I'm not comparing your situation with Thomas cheating on me and having a baby with someone else."

"Okay, but I don't understand."

"You might if you let me finish," I said, my nervousness at what he would do when I told him, making me lash out.

"Continue," he said.

"Thomas and I tried to have a baby, but nothing worked. Then his girlfriend becomes pregnant. And that put it right in my face. I was the reason we weren't able to conceive. I could no longer believe it was because of something else. God, I wanted it to be from anything else. Then I wouldn't have to feel flawed."

"That's what you meant when the condom broke. You said not to worry about it when I panicked a bit. I thought you meant you were on the pill. I was going to ask you, but it slipped my mind with everything going on. You can't think you being unable to have kids makes you flawed, or that it would matter to me."

"It matters to me."

"Ah, sweetheart. I'm sorry. So that is why you were acting weird. You were afraid of how I would react. Christ, I thought you were going to tell me you decided you couldn't deal with my situation with Poppy. Christ, I feel like an ass." Dom chuckled, and when what he said sank in, I got pissed. Any nervousness I had was gone.

"You are an ass. You having a child makes no difference. I fell in love with her the second I saw her. This week was hell. I missed you and her, and I struggled with it because of how fast everything is moving between us. Then I'm not back for two days and start throwing up. I had the workshops to attend, and I had to sit through those with an upset stomach and praying I didn't vomit all over the place. Finally, it dawned on me that I missed my period. I freaked because hello, I thought I can't have kids. The only reason I bought a test is the symptoms fit. Throwing up in the mornings, breasts more tender...no one should search their symptoms on the internet...I also thought I might die from sixty different illnesses and diseases. Thankfully, I calmed down enough and figured the best thing was to rule out things. Hence, buying the test. Once I got home with the test, I started panicking again. I can't get pregnant and when the test shows negative, it would mean I probably had one of the other—"

"River!" Dom said loudly, interrupting me. "Are you pregnant?" he asked after I stopped babbling.

"I was trying to get to that," I said defensively.

"I know. I'm sorry for interrupting you. But I was afraid if it was true, the baby would get here before you got around to telling me," he said and grabbed me, pulling me onto his lap.

"What are you doing?"

"First, I'm going to kiss you. Then I'm going to take you upstairs to my bed. It's been a week. I enjoyed the quickies, but they weren't enough. I want to take my time."

"So... you're okay with the baby?"

"Yep, I'm a multitasker," he said, then kissed me.

After he devoured my mouth, he carried me upstairs and showed me he was a helluva multitasker.

Chapter Seventeen

Jag

Two weeks I'd spent learning baby stuff and if River hadn't been staying with Poppy and me, I wasn't sure either of us would have survived. The experience gave me great respect for single parents. Sami was getting a big hug the next time I saw her. I'm not sure how she handled raising Ally on her own for four years.

As I looked into my daughter's dark brown eyes, I wondered what she thought of our predicament.

"I'm trying, baby girl, but you got to meet me halfway," I said, and Poppy blew bubbles in response.

I looked around the bathroom and cringed. Nothing like a baby to make you feel incompetent.

"So much for surprising River by having you bathed when she gets back from the grocery store." Once again, Poppy's response was slobbery bubbles.

"Are you finished? Can we try the bath again?" I looked at the tub and groaned. Yeah, the only way I was going to get Poppy's bath finished was in the other bathroom.

"Oh my God, what is going on in here?" I turned my head and River stood in the doorway, her eyes taking in the bathroom. "And why are you holding her above the toilet?" she asked as she walked into the bathroom.

Poppy turned her head at River's voice and answered before I did. She still slobbered, but she babbled a string of unrecognizable words.

"I'm pretty sure she's telling you her daddy does not know what he's doing," I said, and River stepped closer, then looked in the tub.

"Oh, Dom," River said, then laughed. "Why didn't you wait until she was finished? You could have drained the tub and washed it out, then refilled it and finished her bath."

"Because it's poop," I said as if River didn't recognize what she was seeing. "I panicked, alright. The poop started coming, and my only thought was to get her out of the water, so I did. And since it was still coming, I kicked the toilet lid up and held her over it. Satisfied?"

River's lips twitched.

"Don't you dare laugh again."

"Sorry, I'm trying to picture you with two," she said, then grabbed the counter as she turned her head and laughed.

"Well, hopefully, Poppy will be using the toilet by the time that one comes," I answered and pointed to River's stomach.

"Dom, Poppy won't even be two years old when this one is here. The chance is slim she will be potty trained unless she takes an interest early."

"Could you at least let me have the fantasy for now?"

"Alright, you can have your fantasy time. Now let me clean the tub out, then I will finish her bath, and you can put up the groceries. Here, let's wrap this towel around her, and I think it is safe to move away from the toilet." I watched as River bundled Poppy in the towel.

"Fine."

"I think your daddy needs a nap, sweetie," River said, kissed Poppy on the cheek, then did the same to me.

I held Poppy while River cleaned up the disaster of a bathroom. When everything was ready, she reached for Poppy. As I handed her over, I leaned over and stole a kiss.

On my way out the door, leaving my two girls to it, I yelled over my shoulder, "When she goes down, I'm going to expect you to tuck me in for my nap." I laughed when the wet washcloth hit my back.

I watched from the doorway as River rocked Poppy and hummed to her while she drank her bedtime bottle. We hadn't discussed what we were going to do since she was pregnant. Getting Poppy settled was the priority. Another reason I hadn't broached the subject was I didn't want to push River. I'd hoped giving her time and showing what we could have together would sway her to my side. Hell, we were already a family of three.

River looked up and smiled when she noticed me in the doorway.

"She's out," she said as she maneuvered Poppy to her shoulder and expertly burped her. When she rose from the rocker and walked to the crib, I stepped into the room. River kissed Poppy's head before she laid her down and covered her with a blanket.

When River walked out of the room with the bottle, I leaned in and kissed my daughter's head. "Love you, baby girl," I whispered, then ran my hand gently over her soft curls. As I left her room, I clicked on the monitor that was on the dresser and pulled the door halfway closed.

Once I was in my bedroom, I stripped down, then climbed into the bed with my back against the headboard. I didn't have to wait long for River to come in.

"Why are you sitting up?" she asked as she walked toward the bathroom.

"Just waiting for you."

"Oh, okay. I won't be long," she said as she went into the bathroom and shut the door. When she came out, she joined me in the bed and positioned herself like I was.

"You know, we need to talk about what we are going to do." I turned my head to face her.

"Yeah, I know," she said, but instead of looking at me, she looked down at her hands.

"How about I tell you what I want? Then you can tell me if you agree or disagree?" I asked, then rested a hand on top of hers.

"Okay."

"We've pretty much been living as a family since I got back. The only time you are at your house is to pick up mail and grab more clothes. I know you love Poppy. I can see it when you look at her. Just like I hope you can see it in my eyes when I look at you."

River's head jerked in my direction. "What?"

"I love you. I will not push you for more than you can give, but I want you to know I eventually plan to marry you." She was going to interrupt, so I put my hand up to stop her. "I also know you aren't ready for that. I'm hoping you will tell me when you are. But I want you to move in here until that time comes. I may have missed the start of Poppy's life, but I won't miss one minute of our child's. You are both mine. Are you going to agree, or do we need to hash this out some more?"

"What happened to agreeing or disagreeing?"

I grinned. "My original plan was to give you that option. But plans change." I shrugged.

"Well, you seem to have it all worked out. Why even ask me what I want?"

"Because it is the polite thing to do." I laughed when she pulled her hand from under mine and smacked my shoulder.

"You can be such an asshole."

"I told you once before, I can. But I'll be your asshole. Now, are you going to agree so I can love on you?"

"You fight dirty, Dom."

"I'll fight anyway I have to—to get you in the end."

When I saw the tear roll down her cheek, under different circumstances, I would have cringed, but then I knew I'd won. Her whispered words validated it.

"Yes, I will officially move in. And you are right. I don't think I'm ready to get married."

"It's on the table. You only need to tell me when you are."

"Okay. Now, didn't you say something about loving on me?"

"Is that your way of telling me the conversation is over?"

"Yes," she said, and I kissed her, then pulled her sleep shirt over her head.

I shifted down on the bed and pulled River with me. After I slipped her panties off, I removed my boxers, then rolled, positioning myself on top.

Leaning on one arm to keep my full weight off her, I used my other hand to trace her nipples. Teasing them as I watched them pebble.

Taking her mouth, I kissed her. She was mine and couldn't imagine my life without her in it. I fought to take it slow, needing to show her gentleness.

I broke the kiss and looked down at her. Her eyes shone with lust.

"You are my perfect match," I said, then gazed down at her firm, round breasts and smiled.

Lowering my head, I ran my tongue over the hardened peak and River squirmed, her body responding to my every touch.

"Dom," she said my name as if it were a plea.

"You need loved slow. We always rush," I whispered and palmed her breast. I loved how it fit into my hand perfectly. After showing each one attention, I moved my hand down. My fingers barely touched her skin as I moved them over to where our daughter or son grew.

River groaned when I reached her mound. As my fingers hit her center, I felt the moisture of her need. Barely grazing her clit, I ran my fingers between her folds, then circled her center before pushing one finger in. As I pumped it in and out, River moved her hips, mimicking every move.

She grabbed my arm that rested beside her and dug her nails in. The bite of pain almost broke my control.

Adding another finger, I increased the speed, curling them to hit the spot that would eventually send her over the edge.

"Please, Dom. I'm close."

I pumped my fingers and used my thumb to press on her swollen nub. River's back arched and her head went back. As I watched her go over, my cock throbbed. I continued with my fingers and thumb and helped her ride out her orgasm.

When she came down, I removed my fingers and positioned the head of my cock at her entrance, and pushed in. She was wet and warm, and I knew I wouldn't last as long as I wanted.

Each thrust, pulling me closer and closer to my release. Not wanting to go alone, I bent my head to her breast and rolled the nipple between my teeth. Driving in as deep as I could go, I gently bit down on the nipple.

River's hand went to my hair, and she latched on as we orgasmed together.

I rolled to the side and pulled River with me until I was on my back with her head on my chest.

"God, I love your tattoos," she said breathlessly as she traced the ones on my chest. "Why is your chest covered except for the blank spot over your heart?"

Grazing my finger up and down her spine, I lazily responded, "When I started getting tattoos, I saved that spot in case I ever took an ol' lady. So I guess I'd left the space for you."

"Dom?"

"Hmm?"

"I love you."

When I said the words early, I hadn't let it bother me when she hadn't said them back. Now I realized I needed to hear them more than anything else.

"Tomorrow, we pack your stuff."

I had gotten her to agree to move in. The next step I could wait for her to accept. As long as it didn't take too long.

Chapter Eighteen

River

Using my heel, I kicked the door shut and leaned the boxes against the wall. I dropped Dom at Soft Tails to handle a problem with the remodel, instead of him getting to come to help me at the house. He said he would get someone to drop him off when he finished, so I wouldn't have to stop in the middle to do it. My plan, though, was to get it all done by the time he got here. Leaving him with the loading of the Escalade.

Between the boxes and the luggage in my closet, I could get all my clothes and personal items packed. The furniture and other household stuff would be dealt with later, per Dom.

That morning, I mentioned renting the house, and Dom told me that Tank, a club member, had wanted to buy it before, but I had beaten him to the punch when Sami had put it on the market. Since Dom would be at Soft Tails and so would Tank, he was going to ask him if he was still interested. As I looked around the house, I hoped if Tank bought it, he'd take some of the furniture off my hands. It would be less to move out of the house if he did. Especially since most of it would have to go into storage, anyway.

Grabbing the boxes, I moved to the stairs. The sooner I started, the sooner I'd get home to Poppy. I'd grown attached to her and hated to be away for long. Though she was in excellent hands with her grandpa. I was thankful when he volunteered to watch her because the packing could take place without interruption. It didn't escape me that I'd thought of Dom's place as home, even though I lived in mine longer. It really was true that people made a house a home. At least for me because I couldn't imagine living anyplace Poppy and Dom weren't at, too.

Pulling out the clothing in the last drawer in the dresser, I placed them in the box and sighed. *Done.* I reached for my cell on the top of the dresser and checked the time and saw the reason for my tiredness; I had been packing for two hours.

Since Dom hadn't shown up yet, I picked up the one empty box that remained and headed for the stairs. My goal, packing the cleaning supplies in the cabinet under the kitchen sink. When I reached the bottom of the stairs and started toward the kitchen, I heard the front door open and close.

"I just finished with my clothes. I'm going to fill this extra box with the stuff from under the sink. Should only take me a few minutes. It's not like we can't use cleaning supplies." Realizing Dom hadn't spoken, I stopped and turned, then dropped the empty box when I noticed the man who was standing in the kitchen doorway, looking back at me.

"Hi, River. You should remember to lock your doors."

"Most people aren't rude. They knock whether or not the door is unlocked. What are you doing here, Thomas?" I asked and stared at the man I had been married to not so long ago. He wore jeans and a button-down shirt that had wrinkles in it. His hair showed signs of where he had run his fingers through it, enough to have pieces sticking up. It was unlike the man who, no matter what he was doing, kept a pristine appearance.

"I wanted to talk with you," he said and took a few steps toward me.

"But I don't want to talk with you. That's why I changed my number."

"Like I couldn't locate the new one. I had the number within days of you changing it. I've been calling, but you have me blocked." Every time he spoke, he took a few steps toward me.

He was right. I'd blocked his number as soon as I changed mine and bought the new phone just in case he found my new number. Knowing Thomas, it explained at least one thing.

"And you felt the need to hire a PI because of it. We are divorced, Thomas. I blocked your number because I have nothing to say to you. I moved here, so I wouldn't even run into you by accident. Why do you think I didn't call you after you had my mother call and tell me you wanted to talk to me? Did you think going that route would make me? I am no longer the woman who goes along with whatever her mother says. And knowing my mother, she would have called you the minute I hung up on her. You cheated, Thomas, and got another woman pregnant. As if that wasn't enough, you blamed me instead of acting like a man and taking responsibility for your actions.

"You have no clue what it was like for me every month to take the pregnancy test and have the results come up negative. When you wanted to start a family, I may not have approved of your reason. No one should have a child to further their career, and it wasn't right for your dad to put that pressure on you. But I wanted a child, Thomas, so I went along. That is on me. So when I confronted you because I overheard whispers of you sleeping with someone on the side, you go into the poor, pitiful me act. *I just needed someone, River, who wanted to have sex with me, and not because they were ovulating.'* Blah, blah, blah. What do you think it was like for me, Thomas? Oh, that's right, it only affected you. Then to find I did everything possible to get pregnant, only to find out I was the infertile one, was the ultimate blow. Because you had no issue getting your girlfriend pregnant. I wanted children, Thomas, and the knowledge I never would hurt. Then I was ashamed because I felt relieved I couldn't conceive because of what you did.

"We married because Alfred, my mother, and your father thought we should. And you and I always went along with what they wanted, so we married for them, not because we loved each other. Things happen for a reason. I never believed that before. I do now because guess what? I can have children. Accept that you and I didn't conceive, because someone or something was watching out for us and didn't want us to make yet another mistake. I've moved on. Be happy with your girlfriend and upcoming baby, Thomas. I'll do the same with Dom… and our child." When I started, I couldn't stop. It felt good to vent at Thomas, liberating, actually. It felt good getting everything off my chest. I knew I had to finally let the hurt and pain go. I might not have been happy with Thomas coming to Shades Valley or even feeling he had some right to walk in my house, but he needed to know I no longer held anything against him.

I hadn't planned to tell him about the baby or Dom, but I needed him to understand that I was happy. I hadn't been in a very long time. And he needed to be, too.

When Thomas pulled out a gun, I realized it had been a huge mistake, along with the fact, I evidently didn't know Thomas as well as I thought.

He lunged, and I screamed.

Jag

"Thanks for the lift. It's been a long time since I've ridden in a sheriff's car."

Will chuckled. "No problem. We were done eating. And if you had waited for one of your men to get freed up with the bar so busy, you'd still be waiting. Or would have had to call River to pick you up," Will said as he pulled out of the parking lot.

"I can't wait to hear the rumors that are sure to fly around town because you know they will. The bar was busy, and people were leaving and pulling in when Will opened the back door of the car and you got in." Carly laughed from the passenger seat. "You really need to let me take a picture before you get out, so I can show Russ."

"No! Because your ass won't just show Crusher. You'll show that shit to the entire club."

"You're no fun, Jag. I thought being with River would relax you and take some of the assholishness out of you." Carly looked over her shoulder, and I flipped her off.

"I'm right here," Will commented, and I grinned.

When River and I told him about the baby, I hadn't been sure how he would take it. Even though he told me I would need to push her, I'm pretty sure knocking her up wasn't what he meant. But like he'd also said, he wouldn't stick his nose in our relationship, and he proved it. He'd taken the baby news in stride, along with River staying at my house and helping me with Poppy.

"Sorry, boss," Carly said.

"Sure, you are, deputy," Will answered, then turned down the street to River's house.

"You can just stop in front of the house and let me out unless you want to come in and see River. You can talk to her, so she doesn't try to help me load shit in the truck," I mentioned because she would try, and she didn't need to be lifting anything in her condition.

"Carly can keep her occupied, and I'll help you load her stuff," Will volunteered as he pulled to the curb, stopped the car, and he and Carly got out.

Carly smirked as she opened the door to let me out.

"It would have made a great Christmas card," she said and closed the door once I was out.

I never had time to reply because we heard River scream. The three of us took off in a run, and as we reached the door, the man's voice told us River wasn't alone.

"You ruined everything because you couldn't keep your legs closed. I should shoot you now!" The man's words were the only thing that had kept me from kicking down the door.

"Sonofabitch," Will said in a low voice, and I looked at him. "It's her fucking prick ex."

"I'll kill the bastard." I turned to the door, and Will grabbed my arm.

"You heard him. He has a gun, and we can't take the chance. You and Carly give me a minute to get around the house to the back. The kitchen door glass might give me a visual of where they are in the house," Will said, leaving Carly and me as he headed to the back of the house.

Carly and I leaned closer to the door when Thomas's voice lowered, and we no longer could make out what he said. Carly batted my hand off the doorknob and grabbed it herself. I put my hand on her arm. No way was I letting her go in first, cop or not.

"Get out of the way, Jag. I am a sheriff's deputy, jackass."

"Yeah, and I don't care," I said and shoved her hand away from the handle, stopping when it gave, and the door unlatched and opened just enough to show it wasn't locked.

"You step in, and I will kill you, then her, asshole," River's ex said, which let us know either Will was at the door, or he was where he could see the front door move.

"Ease the door open a little more. If he's talking to Will, his back will be to us, and we might get inside without him noticing," Carly whispered and pulled her gun out of her holster. "If he was talking to us, you're going to want to be off to the side."

I pushed the door open and we could see Thomas back. He had one arm around River's neck and swung the other arm with the gun between River and Will, who stood at the opened back door.

"Drop the gun or I will shoot you," Will said, his own gun drawn and pointed toward Thomas and River.

"We both know you won't take the chance of hitting your slut of a daughter by trying to take me out. You never liked me, but I'm a hundred times better than some piece of shit biker she's spreading her legs for. I came to take her back since she wouldn't talk to me. We could have made it work once I explained to her that Teresa's baby isn't mine. Seems even my side piece shared her snatch with others, too. Now this cunt gets herself knocked up by some low class—"

"Biker," I finished Thomas's sentence and stepped into the house. I'd heard enough. If he wanted to take a shot at someone, it would be me. But I was done listening to his sorry ass.

Thomas jerk, moved until his back was against the wall and it would allow him to monitor Will and me. His move also allowed me to see River's face. I expected to see fear. Instead, her face was flushed, and her lip was curled. My woman was pissed.

"You're so set on shooting someone. Shoot me, motherfucker," I spread my arms wide, "you know you want to. You can call me any names you want, but I'll still be the man who did what you couldn't do. You aren't man enough for her. You never were. I knocked her up the first time I fucked her, asswipe." Taunting Thomas worked. By the time I finished, his gun was aimed at me.

The next thing was Carly saying, "Shit," as her body slammed into mine and Thomas fired. Carly and I were on the way to the floor when a second shot was heard. I watched Thomas's eyes widen as the gun in his hand dropped and he released his other arm around River's neck to grab his shoulder. Then he did something I would remember as long as I lived. He looked at his shoulder and the hand covered in the blood pouring out of the hole from the bullet and he fainted.

"What a pansy?" Carly said as she and I stood.

"Are you crazy!" I heard River yell and had a second to brace myself before her body slammed into mine. I wrapped my arms around her and held on.

"I'm thinking this damn house needs to be either torn or burned down. More shit happens here than in the rest of the town put together," Carly said, then walked to where Will kneeled by Thomas and talked into his radio.

I had to agree with her. Carly had been attacked by the old VP of the Haven MC, and Crusher had shot him through the window from Sue's place. Now, River.

I held on a little tighter, enjoying the feel of her in my arms. Later, I would think of how easily I could have lost her and our child.

I laid in bed with River in my arms, sleeping while it evaded me. I knew it was because my mind was swirling with everything that happened.

The ambulance had come, and they had taken Thomas to the hospital. He wouldn't be an issue anymore for River with the charges he was facing.

Since he was Will's ex-son-in-law, they would investigate the shooting. Will would come out of it clean, but they would suspend him with pay until it was over.

By the time statements were taken, and the nine hundred people who came and left the scene, it was dark.

River had surprised me through it all. I'd kept waiting for her to break down. It's usually what happened after the adrenaline rush ended for victims of crimes. I said as much to her as we ate dinner. Thanks to my dad who cooked. He was currently crashed on the couch in case we needed him to help with Poppy. I actually think he was just as worried about River as I was.

"I may not have grown up with my dad, but I'm still the daughter of a cop. Everyone came out fine but Thomas, and that's his damn fault. If it had gone down differently, I would have more than likely fell apart," had been River's reply to my inquiry about she looked pissed instead of shaken when Thomas held her with a gun.

The woman made it sound a lot simpler when I knew for a fact it wasn't.

I yawned, pulled River closer, and closed my eyes. In the past, I had some bad luck with women. However, with River in my arms, I fell asleep knowing my luck had finally changed.

Chapter Nineteen

River

It had been my turn to get up with Poppy. The doctors had told Dom to expect a few sleepless nights until she became comfortable with her new surroundings.

As I slid into bed and worked to get comfortable, Dom rolled over and curled around me. His even and deep breaths told me he was asleep. A lot had happened in the short time I'd known him, but as I laid there with him, I wouldn't have changed a thing. He was an important part of the new life I hoped to find.

Dom shifted, and I felt his cock twitch. Maybe he wasn't in such a deep sleep after all. I pushed back against him and stifled the moan that wanted to escape as the arm draped over me moved to slide under the t-shirt I'd worn to bed, then the hand splayed across my breasts. Dom's hand caressed my breast and my nipples turned to hardened peaks. When I felt his lips on my neck, I knew he was awake.

"She go down okay?" he asked in between kisses.

"Yeah, she just needed a dry diaper and a little cuddling. She only took a few drinks from her bottle. I think she's about ready to give them up," I said a little breathlessly. My body had responded to this man from the first encounter with him. It was my head that held me back from seeing what had been in front of me all along. I might not be able to pinpoint the exact second I fell for Dom, but if I had to guess, it was when I noticed him leaning against the hood of my car. Even wearing a ratty t-shirt and grease-stained jeans didn't take away from his looks. If anything, it added to his ruggedness.

Being drawn to him pissed me off, and I'd given him a hard time because of it. I had done to him what I hated most in life—being judged.

Dom placed his other arm above my head and used his hand to move my hair. When he kissed up to my ear and sucked my lobe, I felt my body softening, preparing for him.

My hand moved to the waist of my panties, and I wiggled until I had them down to my ankles, then I kicked them off. Dom groaned in my ear and pressed his harden length into the crack of my ass.

"You ready for me, baby?" Dom whispered, rocked his hips into mine causing his cock to slide up and down the crack of my ass.

"Yes," was the only thing I could force out. The sensation of him pinching and tweaking my nipples along with his cock sliding up and down the crack of my ass was leaving me near speechless.

"Let's see." His hand left my breasts to slide down, and he lifted my leg, pulled it back until it rested on his hip, opening me wide. This time when he rocked his hips, his cock slipped between my thighs and the moisture that pooled there.

Dom kept rocking, and the friction of him sliding through my folds had me growing wetter. His hand moved off my leg, and he positioned it on my mound to where his middle finger rested on my clit. He circled the bud until it hardened and felt as if it had its own pulse. Dom kept the slow and steady pace, and with every pass he made with the finger, my walls contracted. I needed him inside me.

"Dom, please."

"Tell me what you want, baby?"

"You inside me." I wiggled my hips, and the movement captured the head of his cock at my entrance. I tried to scoot down to force him inside, but the slap from his hand he had between my legs stopped me. The slight sting to my clit caused a shiver and forced yet another moan from me.

"Oh no, you don't. I'll give you what you want. Just say it."

"Your cock, I want it inside me, so could you please stop torturing me?"

Dom rolled to his back, and somehow, I went from him behind me, to me on top and facing him.

"I'm a little tired. I think you need to do a little of the work. Ride me, sweetheart. Take what you need."

I pushed up, straddled him, and lined his shaft with my entrance. I lowered, taking him in the position, placing him deeper than he'd ever been. The feeling of being stuffed full was an understatement. Dom groaned when I shifted my hips to get more comfortable.

"You're going to have to move, River. You're killing me," he gritted out. I moved my arms behind me and rested my hands on his thighs to balance me as I used my legs to help me raise and lower on him. The pace was slow at first as I used my wetness to ease him sliding in and out.

The tightness started in my belly and worked its way down to my pussy, causing my inner walls to spasm around him with every downward stroke. Dom's hands latched on my hips and helped steady me.

I knew the second he'd had enough of the slow pace I set. In a fluid motion, he flipped us while keeping our connection.

"I'm no longer tired," he said and moved. Holding his weight off me with one arm, he grabbed my thigh with the other and held it at his hip. With every downward motion, he bottomed out, his balls slapping against my bottom, his pelvic bone hitting my clit.

"I'm close," I moaned out, and he increased his pace. "Dom, please."

"I'll always take care of your needs, sweetheart," he said, letting go of my thigh and pushing forward until he rested on his knees with my legs draped off to each side.

With his hands free, he used them to spread my pussy lips wide, then used the thumb of one hand to press on my clit. When he began the rub in a circle, my walls clenched. I felt the beginning of my orgasm.

"A little longer. Hold it a little longer." His voice showed signs of his own struggle.

No words could explain the feeling I was experiencing. I wasn't going to be able to hold off any longer. My body shook as my orgasm pushed forward.

"Go with me, River!" Dom yelled, pushed deeper, and we went over together.

"I'm never going to complain about getting up in the middle of the night with the kids if this happens when I come back to bed," I said a few minutes later after we could move, and Dom had gotten a cloth and wiped me clean, then himself.

"I aim to please." He chuckled and climbed back into bed, pulling me close.

While laying with my head on Dom's chest, hearing the strong beat of his heart, I thought about why I told him I wasn't ready to marry him. Yet, I moved in with him and Poppy. It was my doubt that it would last, and it would be easier to walk away when it didn't.

But I didn't want easy.

Tracing one of the tattoos on Dom's chest, I whispered, "Dom."

"Hmm," was the sleepy reply I received from him.

"I've changed my mind. Dom, I want to marry you. I love you." I didn't have to wait for his response. He pulled me on top of him, and though his answer earlier implied he was sleepy, the eyes looking at me showed no signs of it.

"Soon, no waiting," he responded. "I want us to be a family in every sense of the word. I love you, too, River."

I leaned closer and kissed his lips as my response. As the kiss deepened, I felt his shaft hardening as it pressed into my lower stomach.

"Again?" I asked as I raised up, breaking the kiss.

"You're the one who woke me up."

"That I did. Now, what are you going to do about it?" I asked, then giggled as he flipped our positions and now laid on top of me.

"I'll show you in a minute. How about getting married at the clubhouse?"

"Will agreeing move us onto the showing part?" I smiled.

"Yes." He grinned back.

"Then a wedding at the clubhouse it is!"

"If this," he thrust inside me, "is all it takes to make you agreeable. Then I'm going to be spoiled getting my way so often," he said, then began to move, leaving me thinking it would be a win-win.

Chapter Twenty

Jag

Lifting Poppy's butt, I slid the clean diaper under before pulling off the soiled one. I learned that lesson the hard way when I changed her on my bed. Not only did I change her, but I also had to strip and clean my sheets. Fastening the tabs, then working the little pants up her chubby legs, I looked around at the men cleaning the yard, arranging tables, putting up decorations. No one who saw the yard would think this was an MC. I wasn't sure I wanted to see inside.

I wouldn't complain because by the end of tomorrow, River would be mine. Once the women heard she had accepted my proposal, and we wanted to get married at the clubhouse, they went into action. On a pleasant note, they'd been able to throw it together in two weeks' time.

"How is it you are the one getting married, but we are putting up the decorations?" I sat Poppy in her playpen that I'd set up in the shade, then looked over at Flirt who stepped down off the ladder where he'd been hanging tiny lights.

"You act like I haven't been helping. I stopped to change Poppy's diaper. You want to do it next time, and I'll keep working?" I asked, tossed the dirty diaper in the big trash can, then picked up another string of lights off the picnic table.

"Uh, let me think about that for a minute... No," Flirt said, moved the ladder, and reached for the lights I held out.

"Brother, if you plan on having kids, you will," Ghost said as he, Coast, and a few of our brothers carried the wood planks for the makeshift dance floor.

"Not if I can help it. I'll bath them, dress them, feed them, but no diaper duty," Devil said as he and Speed walked up with stacks of chairs.

"If I recall, didn't you try to get out of that with Neely?" I asked, then laughed when Devil flipped me off.

"Hey, she wasn't in diapers, and in my defense, I haven't been around small kids. Bailey's gotten me over that, but I'm not sure I'll be able to do the whole diaper thing," Devil said, and I shook my head and chuckled.

"Oh, you will do the diaper *thing,* or this will be the only child you get," Bailey said, pointing to her stomach as she stood in the clubhouse's doorway.

The look on Devil's face, and Speed's whispered "busted," had us all laughing.

"Ah, baby, you know I've got a weak stomach," Devil said as he lifted a stack of chairs and walked toward Bailey.

"Really, you are going to use that? You were a medic, for God's sake." Bailey stepped out and held the door open for Devil and Speed to carry the chairs inside. Devil stopped, leaned in, and planted a kiss on her lips before he went through the door. "You're still changing diapers," Bailey said as she followed the brothers into the clubhouse.

I smiled when I looked over at Poppy playing with her toys and watching the activity going on in the surrounding yard. Every time I looked at her, I couldn't believe I'd only known about her for a short time. And now, I couldn't imagine my life without her in it.

"You're a lucky bastard, Jag," Coast said as he stepped beside me.

"No argument out of me there. Remember when we talked about coming home after we got out of the service?" He nodded, and I continued. "I said something about home and finding the right woman, but, brother, I really didn't expect it to happen."

"Been there, Jag, take it from me. Don't analyze it. Don't break it down and look for loopholes. It isn't a legal document. Just go with it. You've been given a daughter, and a woman who loves you. One who's giving you another child. Grab it with both hands, hold on, and don't look back. Nothing good comes from it," Ghost said, and I faced him to see him folding the ladder behind Coast and me.

"After all this work, your ass better not be having second thoughts," Flirt griped as he stepped down from his ladder and joined us.

"Brother, if you're going to eavesdrop, at least know about what you're hearing," I snapped. "Nothing I said had anything to do with second thoughts. But I have thought about Poppy's mom, Simone. Wondered how things could have ended up differently if she would have moved here with me or I had taken the job offer from her dad. Because I wanted a clean break, it cost me an entire year of my daughter's life. How selfish is that?"

"Jag, that's not being selfish. You broke it off because you knew it wouldn't work out." I glared at Coast, but it didn't faze him, he continued. "Shit happens for a reason, and it doesn't always make sense. If you had done things differently, you would have Poppy, but not River. And sorry, brother, missing out on Poppy's first year was because of her mother's selfishness. You can't tell me you wouldn't have done everything in your power to be a part of Poppy's life if she'd told you about her."

"You know I would have. I'd do anything for her. I'm her dad. She's—" I paused when Poppy started babbling and turned to her. "You giving daddy your two cents, baby girl?"

She'd pulled herself up on the side of the playpen with her face barely visible because of the height of the sides. She bounced on her feet and shook the side of her baby prison. "Da da!"

I froze at her word. It wasn't the first one she'd spoken since I'd brought her home, but I refused to count her repeatedly answering 'no' to everything and anything someone said to her.

"Hey," Coast said and slapped me on the back, "don't think she's talking to us, brother."

Coast's slap to my back and his words jarred me into action, and I moved and picked my daughter up, then kissed her forehead. "That's right, I'm your daddy, and I'll always have your back, baby girl. You can count on it." She laid her head on my shoulder, and I turned around to face the guys. They stood and watched us with smiles on their faces.

"That right there, brother," Ghost pointed at Poppy and me, "is why you don't question the reason things happen." Before I could reply, Ghost walked off and into the clubhouse.

"Shit, I didn't think. He's been so damn happy that it's easy to forget how he was less than six months ago," I said.

"Yeah, Luna's to thank for that," Flirt said.

"The two of you are next," I said and chuckled at the looks my brothers returned. "What?"

"Just because you and the others found women, don't go trying to attach a ball and chain to us." I snorted at Flirt's words.

"Don't you mean placing the ball and chain on your woman?" Flirt's brows lifted, and I knew he was debating on punching me. The only reason he didn't was due to me holding Poppy.

"Or we could always knock a woman up like you guys have. Well, except Crusher." I flipped Coast off, and he laughed.

"Not for Crusher's lack of trying," Flirt added. "Though it will be amusing to watch him try to talk Carly into quitting work when she gets pregnant. 'You know he isn't going to want her on duty with the shit the sheriff's department deals with."

"True, especially after the crap with River's ex. Will got cleared from the mess pretty fast. However, Crusher was none too happy about Carly being involved. Her job or not," Coast added.

Before I could respond, the sounds of bikes had us turning. Poppy raised her head, and I patted her back. Instead of being frightened as the noise grew as our dads came around the side of the clubhouse, she watched and jabbered.

"Look at you, girly, you're not scared of no bikes," Coast commented, and Poppy looked at him and blew a spit bubble, which made us chuckle.

"Why would she? She's got my blood in her veins," I said as the dads pulled to a stop.

As they shut the bikes off, a truck came around the side of the building and stopped behind them with its bed loaded with various size boxes. I grinned when the doors opened, and Thelma and Claire jumped out. Then, for further amusement, I glanced at Coast and Flirt after the two women walked toward Cruz and Romeo and each man threw an arm over the women's shoulders.

"What the hell is going on around here?" Coast mumbled, and I smiled wider.

"Seems obvious to me. Your dads have beat you at finding women." I laughed when both men's head jerked in my direction. "Hey, just calling it like I see it."

"Damn, glad Tank and Bull are working today."

"You think they won't approve, Coast? Who knows, maybe they already know about them," I said, and held tighter to Poppy, who was squirming and reaching for my dad as he headed toward us.

"As protective as they are of their mom, you seriously believe they wouldn't have already said shit?" Flirt chimed in. "After Claire and my dad told Bailey, he told me she approved. I told them she already suspected they were involved, and she was thrilled. Next day, I was coming out of my house when she was headed to work. The woman cornered me and said she'd turn Romeo and me both into eunuchs if he hurt her mom." Coast and I laughed at the look on Flirt's face.

"What are you boys laughing about?" my dad asked as he reached and held his arms out to Poppy. I loosened my hold on her, and she dove into her grandpa's arms. I smiled as I watched him adjust her in his arms, then kiss her cheek. "Has my angel been a good girl?" Poppy babbled as if answering his question. He chuckled, then looked between me, Coast, and Flirt. "Well?"

"Nothing, we were enjoying something Flirt said," I answered. By the look my dad gave me, he knew I was dodging. The other dads and the two women joined us.

"What have you bunch been up to?" Flirt asked.

"Ask him." Romeo pointed to my dad, then continued. "He told us it was a nice day for a ride, then before the rest of us knew, we had the women following us in the truck, and we're at some baby store at the mall. Sly bastard."

"Oh, stop bellyaching," Claire said and smacked Romeo on the chest. "Flyboy needed help with what to buy. Besides, once you and the other men were in the store, Thelma and I thought the truck might not hold all the stuff you kept saying Poppy needed."

"Dad, all that's for Poppy?" I asked as I looked at the boxes sticking up in the back of the truck.

"Yeah," my dad said distractedly as he patted Poppy on the back and rocked back and forth while her eyes blinked sleepily.

"Dad, I have everything she needs at my house."

"Bet you don't have a motorcycle walker," Stroker said, then laughed when I stared at him.

"Seriously, Dad. She is just standing on wobbly legs." I shook my head.

"First, it's cute and my right as her grandpa to introduce her to motorcycles. Second, the shit in the truck is for my place. I want her to have her own things at my house since she will stay with me while you take River away for a few days after the wedding. She shouldn't have to sleep in something called a playing pack."

The other dads agreed with him, and l looked at Coast and Flirt, who shrugged. Thelma and Claire laughed.

"It's called a pack and play," Thelma corrected.

"Don't matter what the hell it's called. My angel isn't sleeping in it. She's going to have a regular crib and all things to go with it in her room. Plus, I'll have it for the new grandbaby, too," my dad said and glared at me as if he expected me to argue.

"Okay, but you didn't have to get it all today. She would have been fine sleeping in the playpen tomorrow night, then after River and I left, you could have stayed at our house with her."

"I want her to get used to my place. I don't want her thinking she isn't welcome there."

"Dad, she's one. Not sure she thinks about much other than food and a dry diaper. And Shakes said she would help you while we're gone."

"I don't need help, boy. I raised you, didn't I?"

"Yeah, and Shakes and some of the other ol' ladies helped. Just call her if you need a break. Okay?"

"Fine."

"Well, since that's settled. How about we go inside and see if they're close to finishing," Preacher said, and didn't wait for any of us to reply. He and Stroker were already headed for the door. The rest of us turned to follow, and I walked beside my dad.

"You want help putting the stuff together?" I asked as I held the door open for him and Poppy.

"Yeah, that would be good if you got the time."

"Always for you, Dad. After I get River settled at Luna and Ghost's place, Poppy and I will come hang out with you."

"Bring what she needs and stay at my place. I'll throw us some food together, then after we get her room set up, we can eat and drink a few beers to celebrate the last night of you being single."

"Sounds good," I said as I walked behind my dad into the clubhouse. It was time to search out my woman. Staying at my dad's place wouldn't be so bad. It beat Poppy and I going back to the house without River being there. After tomorrow, I wouldn't have to worry about it again.

Chapter Twenty-One

River

The sound of the door being opened and closed had me patting under my eyes. I hadn't wanted to explain the few tears that escaped, but as soon as the sound of the footsteps reached me, I knew who it was, and I wasn't going to get out of it.

"There you are. Why're you standing out here? It's almost time."

"Just needed a few minutes to myself, Dad." I forced a smile when he stepped in front of me and hoped my mascara wasn't smeared to give me away.

"Hey, what's wrong, baby?"

I should've known there would be no getting around him; the man was too observant.

"Nothing, Dad. Please don't make a big deal of it."

"If you're having second thou—"

"No… No. I'm not."

"Damn fucking straight you're not." I jumped and whipped around at the voice, and if my dad hadn't grabbed onto my arm, I would have fallen when my heel got caught in the grass.

"For fuck's sake, would it kill you men to make a damn sound instead of sneaking up on people and scaring the living the crap out of them? I swear I'm going to sew bells on all your clothes. No, I'm going to sew a bell on your cut because you go nowhere without it!"

Dom's lips twitched, and he looked at my dad. When I glanced over my shoulder, he was fighting not to laugh, too.

"I'm glad you both find humor in the fact I almost fell."

"Told you not to wear those 'fuck me' shoes, sweetheart. Not that I don't appreciate them or plan to take advan—"

"Stop right there! I know we've had this discussion and if we haven't, well, let's clear it up right now." It was my turn to grin. "Don't you laugh, little girl. I mean it. I don't want, nor do I need, to hear about your sex life. Ever."

"She's carrying my kid. I know you aren't so old you've forgotten how they're made," Dom said, and I elbowed him.

"Christ, son. I swear I'm going to end up shooting you next. And damn, I was just cleared from one investigation for shooting that piece of shit weasel. If I put a bullet in the soon-to-be son-in-law, I'm sure they will take the badge. One, you can write off as a fluke. Two, I'm sure would be considered premeditated. Plus, I don't need the whole club after me. So maybe the two of you can give an old man a break."

"Dad, eventually you are going to have to get over the whole…" I waved my hand around, "…my daughter has sex phobia. I'm a grown woman." At Dad's glare, Dom lost the hold on his laughter. "Oh, come on, I'm going to be pushing a cantaloupe out of my hoo-haw. How are you going to handle that?"

"That's it, I'm going inside. Young people haven't a bit of damn respect for their elders. And I will handle the birth of my grandchild like I handled your birth—in the damn waiting area."

I laughed as my dad headed for the door.

"And, River, nice try deflecting away from the tears you had when I came out."

I glared at my dad's back as he opened the door.

"Enjoy your payback—maybe you'll explain to Dom why you had them in the first place. And for Christ's sake, be careful in those shoes. My grandbaby doesn't need to be jostled around on stilts," he said, then let the door close behind him.

"Between your dad and mine, we might have to fight to spend time with our own children."

When I faced Dom, he was staring at me, and his expression said he was waiting for an explanation. Which I had every intention of avoiding.

"Don't you think so? I mean, he is looking forward to the baby."

Dom cocked his brow, and I knew I didn't have a chance of getting away without talking about the tears my dad witnessed.

"Nuh uh, don't try to distract me with the baby. Give it up, River."

"It's nothing. Really, Dom."

"Well, good. Then you shouldn't have a problem explaining."

"Fine. I came out to get a few minutes alone, and I realized while I stood here that my mother controlled my first wedding and made it into some fairytale—" Dom's frown made me pause. "What?"

"I know the clubhouse isn't what you're used to, but you could have said something when I mentioned it. Instead of agreeing, then crying when the day arrives—"

"Shut up, Dom!"

Dom instantly grew quiet, which for anyone else would be a good thing, but with him, not so much. It usually meant he was gearing up for an explosion. I moved to stand closer to him and reached up and cupped his face between my hands. The muscles in his jaws tightened under my hands, proof he was clenching his teeth.

"Let me finish before you jump to a hundred wrong conclusions. I imagine I had a wedding most little girls dream of having, but it wasn't *my* dream. The wedding was what my mother wanted. It had been just another thing that proved she never knew me, not really. The difference between my parents always makes me wonder how they'd gotten together. Anyway, when I told my dad I was moving here, he was excited and asked me what he could do to help. No questions, no demanding why, and he sure didn't try to take over.

"I made the move for a fresh start, to build a different life for myself. From day one, this place has felt more like home, more like me. Getting to be closer to my dad, and essentially getting to know him better, instead of the man who took his vacation once a year to visit and spend time with me. It's been enlightening, to say the least. Everyone has been welcoming and nice. The women, God, they accepted me into their fold like they'd known me my whole life. I thought I had friends before, but once the divorce was in place, I learned quickly who they were loyal to. It sure wasn't me.

"But the biggest surprise—and the one I wasn't even looking for—was you." I caressed his cheeks with my thumbs and was glad the tightness in his jaws subsided. "The last thing I needed was to get involved. Then there you were in front of me, and I didn't like the feelings you brought on. I fought those feelings, but you just kept showing up. Dom, you didn't just remove the veneer I covered myself in—you ripped it down. You told me once, plans change. And were you ever right."

"Ah, sweetheart—" Dom said, cupped my face in his hands and wiped away the couple of tears that escaped my eyes.

"You know, little girls are misguided into believing the beauty of their wedding day is in the flowers, the perfect gown, twinkling lights, or whatever else they fantasy about to make the day special for them. When only one thing matters—the man who is waiting for you at the end of the aisle. It doesn't matter if he is wearing a tux or jeans and a cut." I smiled and moved one of my hands and placed it on his cut over his heart.

"You're what makes this day special to me. Not decorations or even where we are getting married. And the best part will be tomorrow, then the next day, and every single day after that I get to spend with you. I love you so much, Dom. Thank you for being the man I had no clue I needed."

"Fuck me, you don't ever have to thank me, River. The first day I saw you, you were mine. It may have taken me a bit to realize it, but it doesn't change it. And that's all I give a shit about." Dom wiped more tears that ran down my cheeks, then wrapped me in his arms and bent his head until our lips touched. As the ability to think was about to leave me, I thought every woman deserved their own tattooed, overbearing most of the time, arrogant, and, yes, often rude biker. And I was glad they had earmarked the one in front of me as mine.

The clearing of a throat ended the kiss, and I dropped my hands away from Dom and turned when he loosened his arms.

"Though I can't say I've attended a bunch of weddings, I know the kiss comes last to seal the deal."

"Screw off, Flirt, we're coming," Dom said, then dropped one of his arms and kept the other around my waist to help me on the uneven ground. I was grateful for the support.

"If I'd been a few minutes later, I probably would have seen you two doing just that."

Dom chuckled, and I felt the heat on my face as the blush formed.

"You make it sound like a bad thing, brother," Dom responded, and Flirt snorted when I elbowed Dom.

"Come on, everyone is getting restless, and Claire has already threatened the men that she better not find a finger swipe in the wedding cake's icing, or they would be missing more than their fingers," Flirt said as we walked in the door.

"They better not. I've got plans for any extra icing," I said, and winked at Dom when he frowned.

"What do you need icing for? Are you having one of those weird cravings pregnant women get?"

"Well… no, I just thought…" I lowered my voice, "licking icing off each one of my husband's tattoos would be fun."

Flirt groaned, which told me I didn't quite lower my voice enough. But thankfully, he continued walking without a word. Dom, on the other hand, stopped us in front of Crusher's office door. I'd used the room to get dressed in, and it was where I had left the other women when I stepped outside.

"Go inside. You have five minutes, and this thing starts. Once everything is over, I hope you don't expect to stay and celebrate all night. I'm holding you to the icing remark. And, sweetheart, you know I have a lot of tattoos." Dom winked, and his eyes reflected just what kind of wedding night I was going to have. Then he opened the door and gave me a small nudge. I was through the door, and it was closed before I had the chance to respond.

"Thanks for that visual," Carly said and chuckled while Sami, Luna, and Bailey smiled at me. The old River would have been mortified if anyone had overheard. The new River with friends could have cared less. And it felt awesome.

"I aim to please," I said and moved to grab the hand mirror I'd brought with me to check my mascara. As I looked in the mirror, I hardly recognized the woman who looked back. My eyes were bright, and even I knew it had nothing to do with the make-up and everything to do with being beyond happy.

"I think that is what Jag's counting on," Luna said as she moved beside me.

"Uncle Jag won't really eat all the icing, will he?" Ally asked, and her face held a look of despair.

Luna started touching up my make-up while she and I just grinned at each other. Sometimes it was best to let things go unanswered. But when no one replied, Ally continued.

"If there were cupcakes, he wouldn't get all the icing."

"Stop worrying about the icing and the cake. I'm sure there will be enough for everyone. Now, let me fix your hair and then you need to change your shoes." Sami sat in a chair and pulled Ally between her legs and started working on the hair that had escaped Ally's ponytail.

"But I don't like those shoes," Ally huffed.

"I like my shoes and my dress. They're pretty, right, Bailey?" Neely asked.

"Yes, sweetheart, they are," Bailey answered and smiled when Neely spun while Ally glared at her.

"Geez, I pray these two are boys," Luna whispered in my ear and rubbed her hand over her baby bump.

I chuckled, then whispered back, "I hope this one is, too. Poppy is a handful now. I can't imagine what she'll be like in a couple years."

"At least by the time you have this one, Poppy will be walking. Probably well on to being potty-trained. Unlike me, who will have two the same age," Luna said and set the make-up brush aside.

"You're going to be a great mom, Luna."

"Little late to worry about that now, don't you think?" Carly said, then snorted when Luna lifted her hand, preparing to flip her off, but remembered the little girls in the room and dropped her arm.

"Ally Weston, stop it right now. We discussed this. You are not wearing biker boots with your dress. You wanted to be a flower girl, so there you go," Sami said and reached for the bag that sat on the chair beside her.

"But Daddy gets to wear his and jeans!" Ally said and crossed her arms over her chest. A move I witnessed from the men in the club somewhat regularly when dealing with them.

"Yes, he does. And if you can get your daddy to wear this dress, you can wear biker boots with jeans to the wedding." The room filled with laughter at Sami's response. Even Ally smiled and reached for the dress shoes her mom had dug out of the bag.

We turned toward the door when the knock sounded, then watched as my dad walked in.

"Well, that's our cue," Carly said and stood. Each of my new friends kissed my cheek, and I had to work to hold the tears back. Hormones sucked. I knew the women would be seated by their men once they reached the room, but I was grateful they stayed with me while I dressed. It had kept most of my nervous energy away.

"Sorry, ladies, but there is one impatient man in the front room," my dad smiled and said.

"I doubt it's just one, Will," Carly said, and bent to help Ally get her shoes on.

After the women and children left, I placed my arm through my dad's, and we headed toward the door.

"Ready, sweetie?" my dad asked as we stepped into the hallway that led to the main room where Dom was waiting.

"Yes. More than anything. A little frightened maybe about how quickly I fell for Dom after the ending of one marriage. And I know it looks to the outside that we are marrying because of the baby, but honestly, I would have married him just as quickly if I wasn't pregnant. I love him, Dad. A lot. Which is scary, too," I said as we reached the entrance to the main room and stopped.

"There's your answer, baby. There is not a set time for knowing someone. If it's right, it's right. Dom's a good man. I couldn't have picked a better one to love my baby and take care of her."

"Aww, Dad, you're going to make me cry," I said as my eyes filled.

"Then we better get this thing started," my dad said, and we stepped through the doorway and paused long enough for Ally and Neely to start down the makeshift aisle made by rows of chairs on both sides.

I glanced over the full room to check on Poppy and smiled when I spotted her bouncing on Flyboy's lap. She'd captured her grandpa's heart just as she'd done the rest of us. I might not have given birth to her, but she was as much mine as the one I carried. To look at her now, no one would have guessed that a short time ago, the little girl fought to live. I shifted my eyes back to the front and met Dom's eyes as he focused on me. When my dad squeezed my arm, I knew Ally and Neely had finished their duties and reached the front, which left our turn to take the short walk.

When we reached the front, I released my dad's arm and took the last steps to stand beside Dom. Dom and my dad shook hands, then Dom grabbed mine, and we faced the preacher while my dad took his seat.

The ceremony was short and sweet as Dom and I stood before the club and said our vows. I came to Shades Valley for a fresh start, but I never expected to find the man that would complete me. When the preacher said you may now kiss your bride, Dom kissed me, then pulled back, bent, and pressed his lips to my stomach. I had held the tears off until then.

Dom stood and wiped the tears from my cheeks with his fingers. "Stealing that parking space was so worth it," I said, and everyone laughed as I looked up at him and smiled.

"I knew you saw me!" Dom laughed, and then, before I could blink, he had me off the ground and in his arms. We headed for the door to the outside as whistles and clapping erupted.

Once we reached the backyard, they turned the music on, and it didn't take long for the area to be filled with noise as the clubhouse emptied. Dom set me on my feet in the area designated for dancing and embraced me.

"Love ya, sweetheart," Dom said, bent his head and touched his lips to mine.

"Love you more," I said against his lips.

"Not fucking possible," Dom replied, and I didn't argue as he held me tighter while we moved to the music. I laid my cheek against his shoulder, and he leaned his head down and rested his cheek against the top of my head.

I sighed. I wasn't sure if life could get any better than this. But I was looking forward to every day spent with this man.

Epilogue

Coast

I leaned against the clubhouse and watched the doctor dance with every brother who asked her. I wanted her in my arms, my bed, and my name echoing off the walls when I brought her to completion. It was her I wanted under me when my release took my breath, and my heart pounded in my chest.

Mackenzie avoided me at all costs since the day at the diner when I snapped at her about paying for lunch. I hadn't known then what made me do it, but now, as I watched her head lean back while she laughed at something Bull said, it was because she had the ability to destroy me. I knew it the minute she walked out of her office that day and I had laid eyes on her for the first time. So, I made a play for her. Even now, knowing she could crush me, I wasn't going to be able to stay away from her much longer.

I lost sight of Mac when the music stopped, and River and Jag moved to the front of everyone.

"You boys are falling quick. Been a long time since the clubhouse hosted a wedding celebration. Hell, I think it was when Dare married Shakes."

I glanced at my dad as he leaned against the building beside me, then I turned back to watch River as she prepared to toss her flowers to the women who had formed a group.

"Figure we'll see a few more before long. Maybe we can get the others to do it at the same time," I said, and my dad, Cruz, chuckled.

"Damn, I hope we don't have to break up a bunch of women fighting over flowers."

I shook my head as the group of women laughed and moved around each other to get into the best position. "Thelma's in the group. Aren't you worried she might catch it?" I cocked my brow at my dad.

"You got something to ask me, Emery?"

"Nope, but Bull and Tank might think differently."

"I'll speak with them if the need arises. Only out of respect because they're members of this club and Thelma's sons." I grinned at my dad. "What?"

"Doesn't seem like 'us boys' are the only ones falling quickly. What happened to the *We're going to do what we want, when we want, and enjoy taking off on our bikes whenever the road calls to us'* speech?"

"Still can. Just means we have a warm woman behind us on the bike and in the bed at night when we stop."

"For fuck's sake, don't say that shit to Bull and Tank."

"I getting older, Emery, but I haven't lost any of my brain function."

"Yeah, it isn't your brain I'm worried about, Dad. Now, your ability to move around after they get a hold of you—whole different thing."

"Smartass."

Loud laughter and squeals ended our conversation and had us looking toward the women just in time to watch the bundle of flowers arch and disappear into the middle of the group. When the crowd separated, a grin split my face as Mac held the flowers.

"She's a tough little thing to have gotten in there and come out the victor. Not bad on the eyes either. You know, tradition would put her as the next bride. Be interesting to see who snags the garter."

I looked at my dad, and he smirked. "What the hell does one have to do with the other?"

"See, that's what's wrong in the world today. Young people don't give a shit about traditions."

"Really? I had no clue my dad was a stickler for wedding traditions." I laughed, and he smacked my stomach with the back of his hand.

"You've always been mouthy. I know a lot of stuff. Some are useful, and some are just taking up space in my head." We both chuckled, then my dad continued to share his knowledge. The more he talked, the more my grin spread.

When he was done, I let everything he said run through my mind.

"I think I can work with that."

"I thought you might find it interesting." My dad winked. "And perfect timing for it, too," he added with a chin lift. When I followed the direction he pointed toward, I watched the women set a chair down, then wave River over to stand beside it. They pointed to where they wanted the men to move.

I pushed off the wall of the clubhouse. "Thanks for the chat, old man," I said and walked to where the grumbling and complaining group of men gathered.

"I give this party fifteen minutes to get out of hand once the kids are taken home. Two-thirds of the brothers are already drunk off their asses," Flirt moved beside me and said as he waved his hand in front of us to the group of unattached brothers. Most of them swayed on their feet as they grumbled. Though I found it amusing that not one brother moved from where the women told them to stand.

"It will be good as long as they don't make any fast moves. We could be untangling them for days," I said just as Bull grabbed the back of Tank's shirt as he tilted forward.

"Damn women, I didn't want any part of this." Flirt pointed to Carly, Sami, Bailey, and Luna as they stood in front of the group. "Oh, just do it. He's your brother. It's his and River's day. That was Carly's speech, then Sami's and Luna's eyes watered up because who the fuck knows why. And Bailey, she just points to where I need to go. So yeah, here I am on the outskirts of these drunk bastards."

"Yeah, and bitching like a woman, too." Ghost walked up and smacked Flirt on the back, and I chuckled when Flirt flipped him off.

"Fuck you, Ghost. You're only saying that because I didn't hear them harassing you or the others into this. A matter of fact, your asses scattered when the women started arranging everyone."

"Hey, it's for *unattached* brothers, which we are not. But I'm not ashamed to admit that you are goddamn straight we got the hell away. And I plan to keep away from the women in case they change their minds. Devil mentioned that he, Crusher, Speed, and I needed to restock the bar and coolers before the after-the-kids-leave party gets started." Ghost chuckled and started toward the clubhouse. Where I would guarantee the others were already hiding.

"Sad day when bikers hide from a group of women!" I yelled, and Ghost waved his hand over his head, and never missed a step while he yelled over his shoulder.

"Being a biker ain't got shit to do with it. Having smokin' hot sex later because our women are feeling all romantic and shit—everything."

Flirt and I laughed. He had us there.

"It still surprises me how well he is doing, Flirt." I shook my head as we watched Ghost look around, then slip into the back door of the clubhouse.

"Brother, there were days I wondered if my old friend would ever reappear. I knew he was struggling, and it sucked ass not being able to help him. He couldn't have run into

Luna at a better time. I don't know how much longer he would have lasted if she hadn't come back into his life."

"Our brothers are proof of what a good woman can do for you," I said while I glanced around for Mac and found her standing off to the side.

"If you see that, then what the fuck are you waiting for, Coast? You've never held back when you wanted something. I'm not getting why you're doing it now. Especially if what you want gets you what the others have found."

The whistles and catcalls had Flirt and I facing toward the front of the crowd where River sat in the chair and Jag kneeled in front of her. The sounds resulted because her dress slid halfway up her thigh when Jag lifted one of her legs and rested her foot on his shoulder.

We watched our brother as he ran his hands from River's ankle and up her leg until he reached the garter she wore around her thigh. He popped the band but left it where it was and ran his hands back down her leg. Boos erupted, and Jag turned toward the group and smirked, then turned back, placed his lips at River's ankle and kissed and nibble his way up her leg.

"I'm going inside until this shit is over. One investigation in a man's career is plenty," Sheriff Lance mumbled as he moved past Flirt and me. We waited until he was out of earshot to laugh.

"Hope to hell he isn't packing. Things could get out of hand." I shook my head at Flirt's statement.

"Jag's safe. Will likes him. And I don't think the investigation bothered him as much as knowing the ex-son-in-law still breathes. That pisses him off," I said as hoots and hollers filled the air and grew louder as River blushed and covered her face with her hands.

"Yeah, and it wouldn't look good to kill his grandbaby's daddy."

"There is that," I answered as Jag's mouth reached the garter on River's thigh. He used his teeth to grab hold of it, then worked it down River's leg until he had it off. After, he pulled her hands from her face and kissed her forehead before he stood.

"Sometimes I don't give my dad enough credit," I said, and Flirt looked at me and furrowed his brows.

"For what?" Just as Flirt asked, Jag used his pointer finger from each hand and launched the garter slingshot style into the air.

"Reminding me that traditions are important to keep." I chuckled as my brothers shoved each other around.

"What the hell are you talking about, Coast?"

"That the two sides of me are full of superstitions and traditions." The garter started its descent, and I stepped forward, raised my arm and used my hand to snatch it out of the air. When I pulled back and stood with the garter in my hand, Flirt shook his head.

I looked around until I spotted Mac where she stood with the other women and clapped as Jag lifted River up and carried her off. Flirt and I were silent as we watched the couple stop where Flyboy stood with Poppy in his arms. The baby girl's giggles when Jag leaned in and kissed all over her small face had me smiling.

"How soon do you think before Flyboy is calling Shakes or one of the other women to help with Pop?" Flirt asked while we continued to watch the interaction between Jag and his daughter before he led River toward the houses. They were spending the night on the compound, then leaving in the morning for a few days away.

"The dads handled us as kids. I think Flyboy can take care of one little girl," I said while I focused my eyes back on the woman who had held my attention for months.

"True. Now let's get back to you realizing both sides of your bloodline follow various traditions. From my perspective, it sounds to me like you finally found your balls, brother," Flirt said and slapped my back.

"I never lost them. It just took a minute to remember patience was never my strong point."

Flirt's laughter followed me as I started closing the distance between myself and what I wanted.

Mac.

About the Author

Carson lives in the South with a Great Dane and two adopted shelter dogs that keep the household in line. Books have always been a part of her life. There is nothing better to her than curling up and relaxing with a good story and losing herself in someone else's world for a few hours.

She enjoys writing romance with a real feel to the stories. Writing with the belief not every man is a jerk and not every woman needs saving.

Writing and growing as an author with each book is her goal. She wants to reach the level where a reader knows when they see her name, they can trust there will be a good story as they flip through the pages.

Carson's been on her writing journey for a few years. As she's finally settling in, her only regret is she hadn't started sooner.

To stay up to date with Carson – visit her website-https://carsonmackenzieauthor.com/ or sign up for her newsletter-https://landing.mailerlite.com/webforms/landing/l2k1l8.

Books by Carson Mackenzie

Black Hawk MC

Speed
Crusher
Devil
Ghost
Jag
Coast
Flirt

Haven MC

Moose's Regret
Hawk's Bounty
Keg's Revelation

Desert Phoenix MC

Desert Phoenix Rising

Standalones

Her Way or No Way
two paths One destiny

Boxed Sets

Black Hawk MC Books 1-3
Black Hawk MC Books 4-7
Haven MC Books 1-3

www.ingramcontent.com/pod-product-compliance
Lightning Source LLC
Chambersburg PA
CBHW052039240626
47153CB00006B/2153